THE POOL

OF THE

STONE GOD

AND OTHER TALES

BY

ABRAHAM MERRITT

ISBN: 978-1-78139-236-2

Printed on acid-free ANSI archival quality paper.

The Fox Woman
BY HANNES BOK

Contents

THE POOL OF THE STONE GOD[1]

THIS IS PROFESSOR JAMES MARSTON'S STORY. A score of learned bodies have courteously heard him tell it, and then among themselves have lamented that so brilliant a man should have such an obsession. Professor Marston told it to me in San Francisco, just before he started to find the island that holds his pool of the stone god and — the wings that guard it. He seemed to me very sane. It is true that the equipment of his expedition was unusual, and not the least curious part of it are the suits of fine chain mail and masks and gauntlets with which each man of the party is provided.

The five of us, said Professor Marston, sat side by side on the beach. There was Wilkinson the first officer, Bates and Cassidy the two seamen, Waters the pearler and myself. We had all been on our way to New Guinea, I to study the fossils for the Smithsonian. The Moranus had struck the hidden reef the night before and had sunk swiftly. We were then, roughly, about five hundred miles northeast of the Guinea coast. The five of us had managed to drop a lifeboat and get away. The boat was well stocked

---

[1] EDITOR'S NOTE: This story was first published under the pseudonym W. Fenimore.

with water and provisions. Whether the rest of the crew had escaped we did not know. We had sighted the island at dawn and had made for her. The lifeboat was drawn safely up on the sands.

"We'd better explore a bit, anyway," said Waters. "This may be a perfect place for us to wait rescue. At least until the typhoon season is over. We've our pistols. Let's start by following this brook to its source, look over the place and then decide what we'll do."

The trees began to thin out. We saw ahead an open space. We reached it and stopped in sheer amazement. The clearing was perfectly square and about five hundred feet wide. The trees stopped abruptly at its edges as though held back by something unseen.

But it was not this singular impression that held us. At the far end of the square were a dozen stone huts clustered about one slightly larger. They reminded me powerfully of those prehistoric structures you see in parts of England and France. I approach now the most singular thing about this whole singular and sinister place. In the center of the space was a pool walled about with huge blocks of cut stone. At the side of the pool rose a great stone figure, carved in the semblance of a man with outstretched hands. It was at least twenty feet high and was extremely well executed. At the distance the statue seemed nude and yet it had a peculiar effect of drapery about it. As we drew nearer we saw that it was covered from ankles to neck with the most extraordinary carved wings. They looked exactly like bat wings when they were folded.

There was something extremely disquieting about this figure. The face was inexpressibly ugly and malignant. The eyes, Mongol-shaped, slanted evil. It was not from the face, though, that this feeling seemed to emanate. It was from the body covered with wings—and especially from the wings. They were part of the idol and yet they gave one the idea that they were clinging to it.

Cassidy, a big brute of a man, swaggered up to the idol and laid his hand on it. He drew it away quickly, his face white, his mouth twitching. I followed him and conquering my unscientific repugnance, examined the stone. It, like the huts and in fact the whole place, was clearly the work of that forgotten race whose monuments are scattered over the Southern Pacific. The carving of the wings was wonderful. They were batlike, as I have said, folded and each ended in a little ring of conventionalized feathers. They ranged in size from four to ten inches. I ran my fingers over one. Never have I felt the equal of the nausea that sent me to my knees before the idol. The wing had felt like smooth, cold stone, but I had the sensation of having touched back of the stone some monstrous obscene creature of a lower world. The sensation came of course, I reasoned, only from the temperature and texture of the stone—and yet this did not really satisfy me.

Dusk was soon due. We decided to return to the beach and examine the clearing further on the morrow. I desired greatly to explore the stone huts.

We started back through the forest. We walked some distance and then night fell. We lost the brook. After a half hour's wandering we heard it again. We started for it. The trees began to thin out and we thought we were approaching the beach. Then Waters clutched my arm. I stopped. Directly in front of us was the open space with the stone god leering under the moon and the green water shining at his feet!

We had made a circle. Bates and Wilkinson were exhausted. Cassidy swore that devils or no devils he was going to camp that night beside the pool!

The moon was very bright. And it was so very quiet. My scientific curiosity got the better of me and I thought I would examine the huts. I left Bates on guard and walked over to the largest. There was only one room and the moonlight shining through the chinks in the wall illuminated it clearly. At the back were two small basins set in the stone. I looked in one and saw a faint reddish gleam reflected from a number of globular objects. I drew a half dozen of them out. They were pearls, very wonderful pearls of a peculiarly rosy hue. I ran toward the door to call Bates — and stopped!

My eyes had been drawn to the stone idol. Was it an effect of the moonlight or did it move? No, it was the wings! They stood out from the stone and waved — they waved, I say, from the ankles to the neck of that monstrous statue.

Bates had seen them, too. He was standing with his pistol raised. Then there was a shot. And after that the air was filled with a rushing sound like that of a thousand fans. I saw the wings loose themselves from the stone god and sweep down in a cloud upon the four men. Another cloud raced up from the pool and joined them. I could not move. The wings circled swiftly around and about the four. All were now on their feet and I never saw such horror as was in their faces.

Then the wings closed in. They clung to my companions as they had clung to the stone.

I fell back into the hut. I lay there through the night insane with terror. Many times I heard the fan-like rushing about the enclosure, but nothing entered my hut. Dawn came, and silence, and I dragged myself to the door. There stood the stone god with the wings carved upon him as we had seen him ten hours before!

I ran over to the four lying on the grass. I thought that perhaps I had had a nightmare. But they were dead. That was not the worst of it. Each man was shrunken to his bones! They looked like collapsed white balloons. There was not a drop of blood in them. They were nothing but bones wrapped around in thin skin!

Mastering myself, I went close to the idol. There was something different about it. It seemed larger—as though, the thought went through my mind, as though it had eaten. Then I saw that it was covered with tiny drops of blood that had dropped from the ends of the wings that clothed it!

I do not remember what happened afterward. I awoke on the pearling schooner Luana which had picked me up, crazed with thirst as they supposed in the boat of the Moranus.

THE DRONE

FOUR MEN SAT AT A TABLE of the Explorers' Club—
Hewitt, just in from two years botanical research in
Abyssinia; Caranac, the ethnologist; MacLeod, poet first,
and second the learned curator of the Asiatic Museum;
Winston, the archeologist, who, with Kosloff the Russian,
had worked over the ruins of Khara-Kora, the City of the
Black Stones in the northern Gobi, once capital of the
Empire of Genghis Khan.

The talk had veered to werewolves, vampires, fox-
women, and similar superstitions. Directed thence by a
cabled report of measures to be taken against the Leopard
Society, the murderous fanatics who drew on the skins of
leopards, crouched like them on the boughs of trees, then
launched themselves down upon their victims tearing
their throats with talons of steel. That, and another report
of a "hex-murder" in Pennsylvania where a woman had
been beaten to death because it was thought she could
assume the shape of a cat and cast evil spells upon those
into whose houses, as cat, she crept.

Caranac said: "It is a deep-rooted belief, an
immeasurably ancient, that a man or woman may assume
the shape of an animal, a serpent, a bird, even an insect. It

was believed of old everywhere, and everywhere it is still believed by some—fox-men and fox-women of China and Japan, wolf-people, the badger and bird people of our own Indians. Always there has been the idea that there is a borderland between the worlds of consciousness of man and of beast—a borderland where shapes can be changed and man merge into beast or beast into man."

MacLeod said: "The Egyptians had some good reason for equipping their deities with the heads of birds and beasts and insects. Why did they portray Khepher the Oldest God with the head of a beetle? Why give Anubis, the Psychopomp, Guide of the Dead, the head of a jackal? Or Thoth, the God of Wisdom, the head of an ibis; and Horus, the Divine son of Isis and Osiris, the head of a hawk? Set, God of Evil, a crocodile's and the Goddess Bast a cat's? There was a reason for all of that. But about it one can only guess."

Caranac said: "I think there's something in that borderland, or borderline, idea. There's more or less of the beast, the reptile, the bird, the insect in everybody. I've known men who looked like rats and had the souls of rats. I've known women who belonged to the horse family, and showed it in face and voice. Distinctly there are bird people—hawk-faced, eagle-faced—predatory. The owl people seem to be mostly men and the wren people women. There are quite as distinct wolf and serpent types. Suppose some of these have their animal element so strongly developed that they can cross this borderline—become at times the animal? There you have the explanation of the werewolf, the snake-woman, and all the others. What could be more simple?"

Winston asked: "But you're not serious, Caranac?"

Caranac laughed. "At least half serious. Once I had a friend with an uncannily acute perception of these animal qualities in the human. He saw people less in terms of humanity than in terms of beast or bird. Animal consciousness that either shared the throne of human consciousness or sat above it or below it in varying degrees. It was an uncomfortable gift. He was like a doctor who has the faculty of visual diagnosis so highly developed that he constantly sees men and women and children not as they are but as diseases. Ordinarily he could control the faculty. But sometimes, as he would describe it, when he was in the Subway, or on a bus, or in the theatre—or even sitting tête-à-tête with a pretty woman, there would be a swift haze and when it had cleared he was among rats and foxes, wolves and serpents, cats and tigers and birds, all dressed in human garb but with nothing else at all human about them. The clear-cut picture lasted only for a moment—but it was a highly disconcerting moment."

Winston said, incredulously: "Do you mean to suggest that in an instant the musculature and skeleton of a man can become the musculature and skeleton of a wolf? The skin sprout fur? Or in the matter of your bird people, feathers? In an instant grow wings and the specialized muscles to use them? Sprout fangs...noses become snouts..."

Caranac grinned. "No, I don't mean anything of the sort. What I do suggest is that under certain conditions the animal part of this dual nature of man may submerge the human part to such a degree that a sensitive observer will think he sees the very creature which is its type. Just as in the case of the friend whose similar sensitivity I have described."

Winston raised his hands in mock admiration. "Ah, at last modern science explains the legend of Circe! Circe the enchantress who gave men a drink that changed them into beasts. Her potion intensified whatever animal or what-not soul that was within them so that the human form no longer registered upon the eyes and brains of those who looked upon them. I agree with you, Caranac — what could be more simple? But I do not use the word simple in the same sense you did."

Caranac answered, amused: "Yet, why not? Potions of one sort or another, rites of one sort or another, usually accompany such transformations in the stories. I've seen drinks and drugs that did pretty nearly the same thing and with no magic or sorcery about them — did it almost to the line of the visual illusion."

Winston began heatedly: "But — "

Hewitt interrupted him: "Will the opposing counsel kindly shut up and listen to expert testimony. Caranac, I'm grateful to you. You've given me courage to tell of something which never in God's world would I have told if it were not for what you've been saying. I don't know whether you're right or not, but man — you've knocked a hag off my shoulders who's been riding them for months! The thing happened about four months before I left Abyssinia. I was returning to Addis Ababa. With my bearers I was in the western jungles. We came to a village and camped. That night my headman came to me. He was in a state of nerves. He begged that we would go from there at dawn. I wanted to rest for a day or two, and asked why. He said the village had a priest who was a great wizard. On the nights of the full moon the priest turned himself into a hyena and went hunting. For human food, the headman whispered. The villagers were safe, because he protected them. But others weren't. And the next night was the first of the full moon. The men were frightened. Would I depart at dawn?

"I didn't laugh at him. Ridiculing the beliefs of the bush gets you less than nowhere. I listened gravely, and then assured him that my magic was greater than the wizard's. He wasn't satisfied, but he shut up. Next day I went looking for the priest. When I found him I thought I knew how he'd been able to get that fine story started and keep the natives believing it. If any man ever looked like a hyena he did. Also, he wore over his shoulders the skin of one of the biggest of the beasts I'd ever seen, its head grinning at you over his head. You could hardly tell its teeth and his apart. I suspected he had filed his teeth to make 'em match. And he smelled like a hyena. It makes my stomach turn even now. It was the hide of course — or so I thought then.

"Well, I squatted down in front of him and we looked at each other for quite a while. He said nothing, and the more I looked at him the less he was like a man and more like the beast around his shoulders. I didn't like it — I'm frank to say I didn't. It sort of got under my skin. I was the first to weaken. I stood up and tapped my rifle. I said, 'I do not like hyenas. You understand me.' And I tapped my rifle again. If he was thinking of putting over some similar kind of hocus-pocus that would frighten my men still more, I wanted to nip it in the bud. He made no answer, only kept looking at me. I walked away.

"The men were pretty jittery all day, and they got worse when night began to fall. I noted there was not the usual cheerful twilight bustle that characterizes the native village. The people went into their huts early. Half an hour after dark, it was as though deserted. My camp was in a clearing just within the stockade. My bearers gathered close together around their fire. I sat on a pile of boxes where I could look over the whole clearing. I had one rifle on my knee and another beside me. Whether it was the fear that crept out from the men around the fire like an exhalation, or whether it had been that queer suggestion of shift of shape from man to beast while I was squatting in front of the priest I don't know—but the fact remained that I felt mighty uneasy. The headman crouched beside, long knife in hand.

"After a while the moon rose up from behind the trees and shone down on the clearing. Then, abruptly, at its edge, not a hundred feet away I saw the priest. There was something disconcerting about the abruptness with which he had appeared. One moment there had been nothing, then—there he was. The moon gleamed on the teeth of the hyena's head and upon his. Except for that skin he was stark naked and his teeth glistened as though oiled. I felt the headman shivering against me like a frightened dog and I heard his teeth chattering.

"And then there was a swift haze—that was what struck me so forcibly in what you told of your sensitive friend, Caranac. It cleared as swiftly and there wasn't any priest. No. But there was a big hyena standing where he had been—standing on its hind feet like a man and looking at me. I could see its hairy body. It held its forelegs over its shaggy chest as though crossed. And the reek of it came to me—thick. I didn't reach for my gun—I never thought of it, my mind in the grip of some incredulous fascination.

"The beast opened its jaws. It grinned at me. Then it walked—walked is exactly the word—six paces, dropped upon all fours, trotted leisurely into the bush, and vanished there.

"I managed to shake off the spell that had held me, took my flash and gun and went over to where the brute had been. The ground was soft and wet. There were prints of a man's feet and hands. As though the man had crawled from the bush on all fours. There were the prints of two feet close together, as though he had stood there erect. And then—there were the prints of the paws of a hyena.

"Six of them, evenly spaced, as though the beast had walked six paces upon its hind legs. And after that only the spoor of the hyena trotting with its unmistakable sidewise slinking gait upon all four legs. There were no further marks of man's feet—nor were marks of human feet going back from where the priest had stood."

Hewitt stopped. Winston asked: "And is that all?"

Hewitt said, as though he had not heard him: "Now, Caranac, would you say that the animal soul in this wizard was a hyena? And that I had seen that animal soul? Or that when I had sat with him that afternoon he had implanted in my mind the suggestion that at such a place I would see him as a hyena? And that I did?"

Caranac answered: "Either is an explanation. I rather hold to the first."

Hewitt asked: "Then how do you explain the change of the human foot marks into those of the beast?"

Winston asked: "Did anyone but you see those prints?"

Hewitt said: "No. For obvious reasons I did not show them to the headman."

Winston said: "I hold then to the hypnotism theory. The foot marks were a part of the same illusion."

Hewitt said: "You asked if that was all. Well, it wasn't. When dawn came and there was a muster of men, one was missing. We found him—what was left of him—a quarter mile away in the bush. Some animal had crept into the camp—neatly crushed his throat and dragged him away without awakening anybody. Without even me knowing it—and I had not slept. Around his body were the tracks of an unusually big hyena. Without doubt that was what had killed and partly eaten him."

"Coincidence," muttered Winston.

"We followed the tracks of the brute," went on Hewitt. "We found a pool at which it had drunk. We traced the tracks to the edge of the pool. But—"

He hesitated. Winston asked, impatiently: "But?"

"But we didn't find them going back. There were the marks of a naked human foot going back. But there were no marks of human feet pointing toward the pool. Also, the prints of the human feet were exactly those which had ended in the spoor of the hyena at the edge of the clearing. I know that because the left big toe was off."

Caranac asked: "And then what did you do?"

"Nothing. Took up our packs and beat it. The headman and the others had seen the footprints. There was no holding them after that. So your idea of hypnotism hardly holds here, Winston. I doubt whether a half dozen or less had seen the priest. But they all saw the tracks."

"Mass hallucination. Faulty observation. A dozen rational explanations," said Winston.

MacLeod spoke, the precise diction of the distinguished curator submerged under the Gaelic burr and idioms that came to the surface always when he was deeply moved:

"And is it so, Martin Hewitt? Well, now I will be telling you a story. A thing that I saw with my own eyes. I hold with you, Alan Caranac, but I go further. You say that man's consciousness may share the brain with other consciousness — beast or bird or what not. I say it may be that all life is one. A single force, but a thinking and conscious force of which the trees, the beasts, the flowers, germs and man and everything living are parts, just as the billions of living cells in a man are parts of him. And that under certain conditions the parts may be interchangeable. And that this may be the source of the ancient tales of the dryads and the nymphs, the harpies and the werewolves and their kind as well.

"Now, listen. My people came from the Hebrides where they know more of some things than books can teach. When I was eighteen I entered a little mid-west college. My roommate was a lad named — well, I'll just be calling him Ferguson. There was a professor with ideas you would not expect to find out there.

"'Tell me how a fox feels that is being hunted by the hounds,' he would say. 'Or the rabbit that is stalked by the fox. Or give me a worm's eye view of a garden. Get out of yourselves. Imagination is the greatest gift of the gods,' he said, 'and it is also their greatest curse. But blessing or curse it is good to have. Stretch your consciousness and write for me what you see and feel.'

"Ferguson took to that job like a fly to sugar. What he wrote was not a man telling of a fox or hare or hawk — it was fox and hare and hawk speaking through a man's hand. It was not only the emotions of the creatures he described. It was what they saw and heard and smelt and how they saw and heard and smelt it. And what they — thought.

"The class would laugh, or be spellbound. But the professor didn't laugh. No. After a while he began to look worried and he would have long talks in private with Ferguson. And I would say to him: 'In God's name how do you do it, Ferg? You make it all seem so damned real.'

"'It is real,' he told me. 'I chase with the hounds and I run with the hare. I set my mind on some animal and after a bit I am one with it. Inside it. Literally. As though I had slipped outside myself. And when I slip back inside myself—I remember.'

"'Don't tell me you think you change into one of these beasts!' I said. He hesitated. 'Not my body,' he answered at last. 'But I know my mind...soul...spirit...whatever you choose to call it—must.'

"He wouldn't argue the matter. And I know he didn't tell me all he knew. And suddenly the professor stopped those peculiar activities, without explanation. A few weeks later I left college.

"That was over thirty years ago. About ten years ago, I was sitting in my office when my secretary told me that a man named Ferguson who said he was an old schoolmate was asking to see me. I remembered him at once and had him in. I blinked at him when he entered. The Ferguson I'd known had been a lean, wiry, dark, square-chinned, and clean-cut chap. This man wasn't like that at all. His hair was a curious golden, and extremely fine—almost a fuzz. His face was oval and flattish with receding chin. He wore oversized dark glasses and they gave the suggestion of a pair of fly's eyes seen under a microscope. Or rather—I

17

thought suddenly — of a bee's. But I felt a real shock when I grasped his hand. It felt less like a man's hand than the foot of some insect, and as I looked down at it I saw that it also was covered with the fine yellow fuzz of hair. He said:

"'Hello, MacLeod, I was afraid you wouldn't remember me.'

"It was Ferguson's voice as I remembered it, and yet it wasn't. There was a queer, muffled humming and buzzing running through it.

"But it was Ferguson all right. He soon proved that. He did more talking than I, because that odd inhuman quality of the voice in some way distressed me, and I couldn't take my eyes off his hands with their yellow fuzz, nor the spectacled, eyes and the fine yellow hair. It appeared that he had bought a farm over in New Jersey. Not so much for farming as for a place for his apiary. He had gone in for bee keeping. He said: 'I've tried all sorts of animals. In fact I've tried more than animals. You see Mac — there's nothing in being human. Nothing but sorrow. And the animals aren't so happy. So I'm concentrating on the bee. A drone, Mac. A short life but an exceedingly merry one.'

"I said: 'What in the hell are you talking about?'

"He laughed, a buzzing, droning laugh. 'You know damned well. You were always interested in my little excursions, Mac. Intelligently interested. I never told you a hundredth of the truth about them. But come and see next

Wednesday and maybe your curiosity will be satisfied. I think you'll find it worth while.'

"Well, there was a bit more talk and he went out. He'd given me minute directions how to get to his place. As he walked to the door I had the utterly incredulous idea that around him was a droning and humming like an enormous bagpipe, muted.

"My curiosity, or something deeper, was tremendously aroused. That Wednesday I drove to his place. A lovely spot—all flowers and blossom-trees. There were a couple of hundred skips of bees set out in a broad orchard. Ferguson met me. He looked fuzzier and yellower than before. Also, the drone and hum of his voice seemed stronger. He took me into his house. It was an odd enough place. All one high room, and what windows there were had been shuttered—all except one. There was a dim golden-white light suffusing it. Nor was its door the ordinary door. It was low and broad. All at once it came to me that it was like the inside of a hive. The unshuttered window looks out upon the hives. It was screened.

"He brought me food and drink—honey and honeymead, cakes sweet with honey, and fruit. He said: 'I do not eat meat.'

"He began to talk. About the life of the bee. Of the utter happiness of the drone, darting through the sun, sipping at what flowers it would, fed by its sisters, drinking of the honey cups in the hive…free and careless and its nights and days only a smooth clicking of rapturous seconds…

"'What if they do kill you at the end?' he said. 'You have lived—every fraction of a second of time. And then the rapture of the nuptial flight. Drone upon drone winging through the air on the track of the virgin! Life pouring stronger and stronger into you with each stroke of the wing! And at last...the flaming ecstasy...the flaming ecstasy of the fiery inner core of life...cheating death. True, death strikes when you are at the tip of the flame...but he strikes too late. You die—but what of that? You have cheated death. You do not know it is death that strikes. You die in the heart of the ecstasy...'

"He stopped. From outside came a faint sustained roaring that steadily grew stronger. The beating of thousands upon thousands of bee wings...the roaring of hundreds of thousands of tiny planes...

"Ferguson leaped to the window.

"'The swarms! The swarms!' he cried. A tremor shook him, another and another—more and more rapidly...became a rhythm pulsing faster and faster. His arms, outstretched, quivered...began to beat up and down, ever more rapidly until they were like the blur of the hummingbird's wings...like the blur of a bee's wings. His voice came to me...buzzing, humming...'And tomorrow the virgins fly...the nuptial flight...I must be there...must...mzzz...mzzzb...bzzz...bzzzzzzz...zzzzmm mm...'

"For an instant there was no man there at the window. No. There was only a great drone buzzing and humming...striving to break through the screen...go free...

"And then Ferguson toppled backward. Fell. The thick glasses were torn away by his fall. Two immense black eyes, not human eyes but the multiple eyes of the bee stared up at me.

"I bent down closer, closer, I listened for his heart beat. There was none. He was dead.

"Then slowly, slowly the dead mouth opened.

"Through the lips came the questing head of a drone...antennae wavering...eyes regarding me. It crawled out from between the lips. A handsome drone...a strong drone. It rested for a breath on the lips, then its wings began to vibrate...faster, faster...

"It flew from the lips of Ferguson and circled my head once and twice and thrice. It flashed to the window and clung to the screen, buzzing, crawling, beating its wings against it...

"There was a knife on the table. I took it and ripped the screen. The drone darted out — and was gone —

"I turned and looked down at Ferguson. His eyes stared up at me. Dead eyes. But no longer black...blue as I had known them of old. And human. His hair was no longer the fine golden fuzz of the bee — it was black as it had been when I had first known him. And his hands were white and sinewy and — hairless."

THE FOX WOMAN

CHAPTER I

THE ANCIENT STEPS wound up the side of the mountain through the tall pines, patience trodden deep into them by the feet of twenty centuries. Some soul of silence, ancient and patient as the steps, brooded over them. They were wide, twenty men could have marched abreast upon them; lichens brown and orange traced strange symbols on their grey stones, and emerald mosses cushioned them. At times the steps climbed steep as stairs, and at times they swept leisurely around bastions of the mountain, but always on each side the tall pines stood close, green shoulder to shoulder, vigilant.

At the feet of the pines crouched laurels and dwarfed rhododendrons of a singular regularity of shape and of one height, that of a kneeling man. Their stiff and glossy leaves were like links on coats-of-mail...like the jade-lacquered scale-armor of the Green Archers of Kwanyin who guard the goddess when she goes forth in the Spring to awaken the trees. The pines were like watchful sentinels, and oddly like crouching archers were the laurels and the dwarfed rhododendrons, and they said as plainly as though with tongues: Up these steps you may go, and down them — but never try to pass through us!

A woman came round one of the bastions. She walked stubbornly, head down, as one who fights against a strong wind — or as one whose will rides, lashing the reluctant body on. One white shoulder and breast were bare, and on the shoulder was a bruise and blood, four scarlet streaks above the purpled patch as though a long-nailed hand had struck viciously, clawing. And as she walked she wept.

The steps began to lift. The woman raised her head and saw how steeply here they climbed. She stopped, her hands making little fluttering helpless motions.

She turned, listening. She seemed to listen not with ears alone but with every tensed muscle, her entire body one rapt chord of listening through which swept swift arpeggios of terror. The brittle twilight of the Yunnan highlands, like clearest crystal made impalpable, fell upon brown hair shot with gleams of dull copper, upon a face lovely even in its dazed horror. Her grey eyes stared down the steps, and it was as though they, too, were listening rather than seeing…

She was heavy with child…

She heard voices beyond the bend of the bastion, voices guttural and sing-song, angry and arguing, protesting and urging. She heard the shuffle of many feet, hesitating, halting, but coming inexorably on. Voices and feet of the hung-hutzes, the outlaws who had slaughtered her husband and Kenwood and their bearers a scant hour ago, and who but for Kenwood would now have her. They had found her trail.

She wanted to die; desperately Jean Meredith wanted to die; her faith taught her that then she would rejoin that scholarly, gentle lover-husband of hers whom she had loved so dearly although his years had been twice her own. It would not matter did they kill her quickly, but she knew they would not do that. And she could not endure even the thought of what must befall her through them before death came. Nor had she weapon to kill herself. And there was that other life budding beneath her heart.

But stronger than desire for death, stronger than fear of torment, stronger than the claim of the unborn was something deep within her that cried for vengeance. Not vengeance against the hung-hutzes—they were only a pack of wild beasts doing what was their nature to do. This cry was for vengeance against those who had loosed them, directed them. For this she knew had been done, although how she knew it she could not yet tell. It was not accident, no chance encounter that swift slaughter. She was sure of that.

It was like a pulse, that cry for vengeance; a pulse whose rhythm grew, deadening grief and terror, beating strength back into her. It was like a bitter spring welling up around her soul. When its dark waters had risen far enough they would touch her lips and she would drink of them...and then knowledge would come to her...she would know who had planned this evil thing, and why. But she must have time—time to drink of the waters— time to learn and avenge. She must live...for vengeance...

Vengeance is mine, saith the Lord!

It was as though a voice had whispered the old text in her ear. She struck her breast with clenched hands; she looked with eyes grown hard and tearless up to the tranquil sky; she answered the voice:

"A lie! Like all the lies I have been taught of—You! I am through with—You! Vengeance! Whoever gives me vengeance shall be my God!"

The voices and the feet were nearer. Strange, how slowly, how reluctantly they advanced. It was as though they were afraid. She studied the woods beyond the pines. Impenetrable; or if not, then impossible for her. They would soon find her if she tried to hide there. She must go on—up the steps. At their end might be some hiding place…perhaps sanctuary…

Yes, she was sure the hung-hutzes feared the steps… they came so slowly, so haltingly…arguing, protesting…

She had seen another turn at the top of this steep. If she could reach it before they saw her, it might be that they would follow her no further. She turned to climb…

A fox stood upon the steps a dozen feet above her, watching her, barring her way. It was a female fox, a vixen. Its coat was all silken russet-red. It had a curiously broad head and slanted green eyes. On its head was a mark, silver white and shaped like the flame of a candle wavering in the wind.

The fox was lithe and graceful, Jean Meredith thought, as a dainty woman. A mad idea came, born of her despair and her denial of that God whom she had been taught from childhood to worship as all-good, all-wise, all-powerful. She thrust her hands out to the fox. She cried to it:

"Sister—you are a woman! Lead me to safety that I may have vengeance—sister!"

Remember, she had just seen her husband die under the knives of the hung-hutzes and she was with child… and who can know upon what fantastic paths of unreality a mind so beset may stray.

As though it had understood the fox paced slowly down the steps. And again she thought how like a graceful woman it was. It paused a little beyond reach of her hand, studying her with those slanted green eyes—eyes clear and brilliant as jewels, sea-green, and like no eyes she had ever seen in any animal. There seemed faint mockery in their gaze, a delicate malice, but as they rested upon her bruised shoulder and dropped to her swollen girdle, she could have sworn that there was human comprehension in them, and pity. She whispered:

"Sister—help me!"

There was a sudden outburst of the guttural singsong. They were close now, her pursuers, close to the bend of the steps round which she had come. Soon they must turn it and see her. She stood staring at the fox expectantly…hoping she knew not what.

The fox slipped by her, seemed to melt in the crouching bushes. It vanished.

Black despair, the despair of a child who finds itself abandoned to wild beasts by one it has trusted, closed in on Jean Meredith. What she had hoped for, what she had expected of help, was vague, unformulated. A miracle by alien gods, now she had renounced her own? Or had her appeal to the vixen deeper impulse? Atavistic awakenings, anthropomorphic, going back to that immemorial past when men first thought of animals and birds as creatures with souls like theirs, but closer to Nature's spirit; given by that spirit a wisdom greater than human, and more than human powers—servants and messengers of potent deities and little less than gods themselves.

Nor has it been so long ago that St. Francis of Assisi spoke to the beasts and birds as he did to men and women, naming them Brother Wolf and Brother Eagle. And did not St. Conan baptize the seals of the Orkneys as he did the pagan men? The past and all that men have thought in the past is born anew within us all. And sometimes strange doors open within our minds—and out of them or into them strange spirits come or go. And whether real or unreal, who can say?

The fox seemed to understand—had seemed to promise—something. And it had abandoned her, fled away! Sobbing, she turned to climb the steps.

Too late! The hung-hutzes had rounded the bend.

There was a howling chorus. With obscene gestures, yapping threats, they ran toward her. Ahead of the pack was the pock-faced, half-breed Tibetan leader whose knife had been the first to cut her husband down. She watched them come, helpless to move, unable even to close her eyes. The pock-face saw and understood, gave quick command, and the pack slowed to a walk, gloating upon her agony, prolonging it.

They halted! Something like a flicker of russet flame had shot across the steps between her and them. It was the fox. It stood there, quietly regarding them. And hope flashed up through Jean Meredith, melting the cold terror that had frozen her. Power of motion returned. But she did not try to run. She did not want to run. The cry for vengeance was welling up again. She felt that cry reach out to the fox.

As though it had heard her, the fox turned its head and looked at her. She saw its green eyes sparkle, its white teeth bared as though it smiled.

Its eyes withdrawn, the spell upon the hung-hutzes broke. The leader drew pistol, fired upon the fox.

Jean Meredith saw, or thought she saw, the incredible.

Where fox had been, stood now a woman! She was tall, and lithe as a young willow. Jean Meredith could not see her face, but she could see hair of russet-red coifed upon a small and shapely head. A silken gown of russet-red, sleeveless, dropped to the woman's feet. She raised an arm and pointed at the pock-faced leader. Behind him his men

were silent, motionless, even as Jean Meredith had been—
and it came to her that it was the same ice of terror that
held them. Their eyes were fixed upon the woman.

The woman's hand dropped—slowly. And as it
dropped, the pock-faced Tibetan dropped with it. He sank
to his knees and then upon his hands. He stared into her
face, lips drawn back from his teeth like a snarling dog,
and there was foam upon his lips. Then he hurled himself
upon his men, like a wolf. He sprang upon them howling;
he leaped up at their throats, tearing at them with teeth
and talons. They milled, squalling rage and bewildered
terror. They tried to beat him off—they could not.

There was a flashing of knives. The pock-face lay
writhing on the steps, like a dog dying. Still squalling,
never looking behind them, his men poured down the
steps and away.

Jean Meredith's hands went up, covering her eyes. She
dropped them—a fox, all silken russet-red, stood where
the woman had been. It was watching her. She saw its
green eyes sparkle, its white teeth bared as though it
smiled—it began to walk daintily up the steps toward her.

Weakness swept over her; she bent her head, crumpled
to her knees, covered again her eyes with shaking hands.
She was aware of an unfamiliar fragrance—disturbing,
evocative of strange, fleeting images. She heard low, sweet
laughter. She heard a soft voice whisper:

"Sister!"

She looked up. A woman's face was bending over her. An exquisite face...with sea-green, slanted eyes under a broad white brow...with hair of russet-red that came to a small peak in the center of that brow...a lock of silvery white shaped like the flame of a candle wavering in the wind...a nose long but delicate, the nostrils slightly flaring, daintily...a mouth small and red as the royal coral, heart-shaped, lips full, archaic.

Over that exquisite face, like a veil, was faint mockery, a delicate malice that had in them little of the human. Her hands were white and long and slender.

They touched Jean Meredith's heart...soothing her, strengthening her, drowning fear and sorrow.

She heard again the sweet voice, lilting, faintly amused—with the alien, half-malicious amusement of one who understands human emotion yet has never felt it, but knows how little it matters:

"You shall have your vengeance—Sister!" The white hands touched her eyes...she forgot... and forgot...and now there was nothing to remember...not even herself...

It seemed to Jean Meredith that she lay cushioned within soft, blind darkness—illimitable, impenetrable. She had no memories; all that she knew was that she was. She thought: I am I. The darkness that cradled her was gentle, kindly. She thought: I am a spirit still unborn in the womb of night. But what was night...and what was spirit? She thought: I am content—I do not want to be born again. Again? That meant that she had been born before...a word came to her—Jean. She thought: I am Jean...but who was Jean?

She heard two voices speaking. One a woman's, soft and sweet with throbbing undertones like plucked harp strings. She had heard that voice before...before, when she had been Jean. The man's voice was low, filled with tranquillity, human...that was it, the voice held within it a humanness the sweet voice of the woman lacked. She thought: I, Jean, am human...

The man said: "Soon she must awaken. The tide of sleep is high on the shore of life. It must not cover it."

The woman answered: "I command that tide. And it has begun to ebb. Soon she will awaken."

He asked: "Will she remember?"

The woman said: "She will remember. But she will not suffer. It will be as though what she remembers had happened to another self of hers. She will pity that self, but it will be to her as though it died when died her husband. As indeed it did. That self bears the sorrow, the pain, the agony. It leaves no legacy of them to her—save memory."

And now it seemed to her that for a time there was a silence...although she knew that time could not exist within the blackness that cradled her...and what was—time?

The man's voice broke that silence, musingly: "With memory there can be no happiness for her, long as she lives."

The woman laughed, a tingling-sweet mocking chime: "Happiness? I thought you wiser than to cling to that illusion, priest. I give her serenity, which is far better than happiness. Nor did she ask for happiness. She asked for vengeance. And vengeance she shall have."

The man said: "But she does not know who—"

The woman interrupted: "She does know. And I know. And so shall you when you have told her what was wrung from the Tibetan before he died. And if you still do not believe, you will believe when he who is guilty comes here, as come he will—to kill the child."

The man whispered: "To kill the child!"

The woman's voice became cold, losing none of its sweetness but edged with menace: "You must not let him have it, priest. Not then. Later, when the word is given you..."

Again the voice grew mocking..."I contemplate a journey...I would see other lands, who so long have dwelt among these hills...and I would not have my plans spoiled by precipitancy..." Once more Jean Meredith heard the tingling laughter. "Have no fear, priest. They will help you—my sisters."

He said, steadily: "I have no fear."

The woman's voice became gentle, all mockery fled. She said:

"I know that, you who have had wisdom and courage to open forbidden doors. But I am bound by a threefold cord—a promise, a vow, and a desire. When a certain time comes, I must surrender much—must lie helpless, bound by that cord. It is then that I shall need you, priest, for this man who will come…"

The voices faded. Slowly the blackness within which she lay began to lighten. Slowly, slowly, a luminous greyness replaced it. She thought, desperately: I am going to be born! I don't want to be born! Implacably, the light increased. Now within the greyness was a nimbus of watery emerald. The nimbus became brighter, brighter…

She was lying upon a low bed, in a nest of silken cushions. Close to her was an immense and ancient bronze vessel, like a baptismal font. The hands of thousands of years had caressed it, leaving behind them an ever deepening patina like a soft green twilight. A ray of the sun shone upon it, and where the ray rested, the patina gleamed like a tiny green sun. Upon the sides of the great bowl were strange geometric patterns, archaic, the spirals and meanders of the Lei-wen—the thunder patterns. It stood upon three legs, tripodal…why, it was the ancient ceremonial vessel, the Tang font which Martin had brought home from Yunnan years ago…and she was back home…she had dreamed that she had been in China and that Martin…that Martin…

She sat up abruptly and looked through wide, opened doors into a garden. Broad steps dropped shallowly to an oval pool around whose sides were lithe willows trailing green tendrils in the blue water, wisterias with drooping ropes of blossoms, white and pale azure, and azaleas like flower flames. Rosy lilies lay upon the pool's breast. And at its far end was a small pagoda, fairy-like, built all of tiles of iridescent peacock blue and on each side a stately cypress, as though they were its ministers...why, this was their garden, the garden of the blue pagoda which Martin had copied from that place in Yunnan where lived his friend, the wise old priest...

But there was something wrong. These mountains were not like those of the ranch. They were conical, their smooth bare slopes of rose-red stone circled with trees...they were like huge stone hats with green brims...

She turned again and looked about the room. It was a wide room and a deep one, but how deep she could not see, because the sun streaming in from a high window struck the ancient vessel and made a curtain, veiling it beyond. She could see that there were beams across its ceiling, mellow with age, carved with strange symbols. She caught glimpses of ivory and of gleaming lacquer. There was a low altar of what seemed green jade, curiously carved and upon which were ceremonial objects of unfamiliar shape, a huge ewer of bronze whose lid was the head of a fox...

A man came toward her, walking out of the shadows beyond the ancient Tang vessel. He was clothed from neck to feet in a silken robe of silvery-blue upon which were embroidered, delicately as though by spiders, Taoist symbols and under them, ghostly in silver threads, a fox's head. He was bald, his face heavy, expressionless, skin smooth and faded yellow as some antique parchment. So far as age went he might have been sixty — or three hundred. But it was his eyes that held Jean Meredith. They were large and black and, liquid, and prodigiously alive. They were young eyes, belying the agelessness of the heavy face; and it was as though the face was but a mask from which the eyes had drawn all life into themselves. They poured into her strength and calmness and reassurance, and from her mind vanished all vagueness, all doubts, all fears. Her mind for the first time since the ambush was clear, crystal clear, her thoughts her own.

She remembered — remembered everything. But it was as though all had happened to another self. She felt pity for that self, but it had left no heritage of sorrow. She was tranquil. The black, youthful eyes poured tranquillity into her.

She said: "I know you. You are Yu Ch'ien, the wise priest my husband loved. This is the Temple of the Foxes."

CHAPTER II

"I AM YU CH'IEN, my daughter." His voice was the man's voice which she had heard when cradled in the darkness.

She tried to rise, then swayed back upon the bed, weakness overcoming her.

He said: "A night and a day, and still another night and half this day you have slept, and now you must eat." He spoke the English words slowly, as one whose tongue had long been stranger to them.

He clapped his hands and a woman slipped by the great vase through the bars of the sunlight. She was ageless as he, with broad shrewd face and tilted sloeblack eyes that were kindly yet very wise. A smock covered her from full breasts to knees, and she was sturdy and strong and brown as though she had been carved from seasoned wood. In her hands was a tray upon which was a bowl of steaming broth and oaten cakes.

The woman sat beside Jean Meredith, lifting her head, resting it against her deep bosom and feeding her like a child, and now Jean saw that herself was naked except for a thin robe of soft blue silk and that upon it was the moon-silver symbol of the fox.

The priest nodded, his eyes smiled upon her. "Fienwi will attend you. Soon you will be stronger. Soon I shall return. Then we shall talk."

He passed out of the wide doors. The woman fed her the last of the broth, the last of the little cakes. She left her, and returned with bowls of bronze in which was water hot and cold; undressed her; ministered to her, bathed her and rubbed her; dressed her in fresh silken robes of blue; strapped sandals to her feet, and smiling, left her. Thrice Jean essayed to speak to her, but the woman only shook her head, answering in a lisping dialect, no sound of which she recognized.

The sun had moved from the great Tang font. She lay back, lazily. Her mind was limpidly clear; upon it was reflected all through which she had passed, yet it was tranquil, untroubled, like a woodland pool that reflects the storm clouds but whose placid surface lies undisturbed. The things that had happened were only images reflected upon her mind. But under that placid surface was something implacable, adamant-hard, something that would have been bitter did it not know that it was to be satisfied.

She thought over what Martin had told her of Yu Ch'ien. A Chinese whose forefathers had been enlightened rulers ten centuries before the Man of Galilee had been raised upon the cross, who had studied Occidental thought both in England and France, and had found little in it to satisfy his thirst for wisdom; who had gone back to the land of his fathers, embraced at last the philosophy of Lao-Tse, and had withdrawn from the world to an ancient fane in Yunnan known as the Temple of the Foxes, a temple reverenced and feared and around which strange legends clustered; there to spend his life in meditation and study.

What was it Martin had called him? Ah, yes, a master of secret and forgotten knowledge, a master of illusion. She knew that of all men, Martin had held Yu Ch'ien in profoundest respect, deepest affection...she wondered if the woman she had seen upon the steps had been one of his illusions...if the peace she felt came from him...if he had made sorrow and pain of soul illusions for her...and was she thinking the thoughts he had placed in her mind—or her own...she wondered dreamily, not much caring...

He came through the doors to her, and again it was as though his eyes were springs of tranquillity from which her soul drank deep. She tried to rise, to greet him; her mind was strong but through all her body was languor. He touched her forehead, and the languor fled. He said:

"All is well with you, my daughter. But now we must talk. We will go into the garden."

He clapped his hands. The brown woman, Fienwi, came at the summons, and with her two blue-smocked men bearing a chair. The woman lifted her, placed her in the chair. The men carried her out of the wide doors, down the shallow steps to the blue pool. She looked behind her as she went.

The temple was built into the brow of the mountain. It was of brown stone and brown wood. Slender pillars hard bitten by the teeth of the ages held up a curved roof of the peacock blue tiles. From the wide doors through which she had come a double row of sculptured foxes ran, like Thebes' road of the Sphynxes, half way down to the pool. Over the crest of the mountain crept the ancient steps up which she had stumbled. Where the steps joined the temple, stood a tree covered all with white blossoms. It wavered in the wind like the flame of a candle.

Strangely was the temple like the head of a fox, its muzzle between the paws of the rows of sculptured foxes, the crest of the mountain its forehead and the white blossoming tree, like the lock of white upon the forehead of the fox of the steps...and the white lock upon the forehead of the woman...

They were at the pool. There was a seat cut at the end, facing the blue pagoda. The woman Fienwi piled the stone with cushions and, as she waited, Jean Meredith saw that there were arms to this seat and that at the end of each was the head of a fox, and that over its back was a tracery of dancing foxes; and she saw, too, that on each side of the seat tiny paths had been cut in stone leading to the water, as though for some small-footed creatures to trot upon and drink.

She was lifted to the stone chair, and sank into the cushions. Except for the seat and the little runways, it was as though she sat beside the pool Martin had built at their California ranch. There, as here, the willows dipped green tendrils into the water; there, as here, drooped ropes of wisteria, pale amethyst and white. And here as there was peace.

Yu Ch'ien spoke: "A stone is thrown into a pool. The ripples spread and break against the shore. At last they cease and the pool is as before. Yet when the stone strikes, as it sinks and while the ripples live, microscopic lives within the pool are changed. But not for long. The stone touches bottom, the pool again becomes calm. It is over, and life for the tiny things is as before."

She said quietly, out of the immense clarity of her mind: "You mean, Yu Ch'ien, that my husband's murder was such a stone."

He went on, as though she had not spoken: "But there is life within life, and over life, and under life—as we know life. And that which happens to the tiny things within the pool may be felt by those beneath and above them. Life is a bubble in which are lesser bubbles which we cannot see, and the bubble we call life is only part of a greater bubble which also we may not see. But sometimes we perceive those bubbles, sometimes glimpse the beauty of the greater, sense the kinship of the lesser...and sometimes a lesser life touches ours and then we speak of demons...and when the greater ones touch us we name it inspiration from Heaven, an angel speaking through our lips—"

She interrupted, thought crystal clear: "I understand you, Martin's murder was the stone. It would pass with its ripples—but it has disturbed some pool within which it was a lesser pool. Very well, what then?"

He said: "There are places in this world where the veil between it and the other worlds is thin. They can enter. Why it is so, I do not know—but I know it is so. The ancients recognized such places. They named those who dwelt unseen there the genii locorum—literally, the spirits of the places. This mountain, this temple, is such a place. It is why I came to it."

She said: "You mean the fox I saw upon the steps. You mean the woman I thought I saw take the place of that fox, and who drove the Tibetan mad. The fox I asked to help me and to give me revenge, and whom I called sister. The woman I thought I saw who whispered to me that I should have revenge and who called me sister. Very well, what then?"

He answered: "It is true. The murder of your husband was the stone. Better to have let the ripples die. But there was this place...there was a moment...and now the ripples cannot die until—"

Again she interrupted the true thought—or what she believed the true thought—flashing up through her mind like sun-glints from jewels at a clear pool's bottom. "I had denied my God. Whether he exists or does not, I had stripped myself of my armor against those other lives. I did it where and when such other lives, if they exist, could strike. I accept that. And again, what then?"

He said: "You have a strong soul, my daughter."

She answered, with a touch of irony: "While I was within the blackness, before I awakened, I seemed to hear two persons talking, Yu Ch'ien. One had your voice, and the other the voice of the fox woman who called me sister. She promised me serenity. Well, I have that. And having it, I am as unhuman as was her voice. Tell me, Yu Ch'ien, whom my husband called master of illusions, was that woman upon the steps one of your illusions, and was her voice another? Does my serenity come from her or from you? I am no child, and, I know how easily you could accomplish this, by drugs or by your will while I lay helpless."

He said: "My daughter, if they were illusions—they were not mine. And if they were illusions, then I, like you, am victim to them."

She asked: "You mean you have seen—her?"

He answered: "And her sisters. Many times."

She said shrewdly: "Yet that does not prove her real—she might have passed from your mind to mine."

He did not answer. She asked abruptly: "Shall I live?"

He replied without hesitation. "No."

She considered that for a little, looking at the willow tendrils, the ropes of wisteria. She mused: "I did not ask for happiness, but she gives me serenity. I did not ask for life, so she gives me—vengeance. But I no longer care for vengeance."

He said gravely: "It does not matter. You struck into that other life. You asked, and you were promised. The ripples upon the greater pool cannot cease until that promise is fulfilled."

She considered that, looking at the conical hills. She laughed. "They are like great stone hats with brims of green. What are their faces like, I wonder." He asked: "Who killed your husband?" She answered, still smiling at the hatted hills: "Why, his brother, of course."

He asked: "How do you know that?"

She lifted her arms and twined her hands behind her neck. She said, as impersonally as though she read from a book: "I was little more than twenty when I met Martin, Just out of college. He was fifty. But inside—he was a dreaming boy. Oh, I knew he had lots and lots of money. It didn't matter. I loved him—for the boy inside him. He asked me to marry him. I married him.

"Charles hated me from the beginning. Charles is his brother, fifteen years younger. Charles' wife hated me. You see, there was no other besides Charles until I came. If Martin died—well, all his money would go to Charles. They never thought he would marry. For the last ten years Charles had looked after his business—his mines, his investments. I really don't blame Charles for hating me—but he shouldn't have killed Martin.

"We spent our honeymoon out on Martin's ranch. He has a pool and garden just like this, you know. It's just as beautiful, but the mountains around it have snowy caps instead of the stony, green-rimmed ones. And he had a great bronze vessel like that of yours. He told me that he had copied the garden from Yu Ch'ien's even to the blue pagoda. And that the vessel had a mate in Yu Ch'ien's Temple of the Foxes. And he told me...of you..."

"Then the thought came to him to return to you and your temple. Martin was a boy—the desire gripped him. I did not care, if it made him happy. So we came.

"Charles came with us as far as Nanking. Hating me, I knew, every mile of the journey. At Nanking—I told Martin I was going to have a baby. I had known it for months but I hadn't told him because I was afraid he would put off this trip on which he had set his heart. Now I knew I couldn't keep it secret much longer. Martin was so happy! He told Charles, who hated me then more than ever. And Martin made a will. If Martin should die,

Charles was to act as trustee for me and the child, carry on the estate as before, with his share of the income increased. All the balance, and there are millions, was left to me and the coming baby. There was also a direct bequest of half a million to Charles.

"Martin read the will to him. I was present. So was Kenwood, Martin's secretary. I saw Charles turn white, but outwardly he was pleasantly acquiescent, concerned only lest something really might happen to his brother. But I guessed what was in his heart.

"Kenwood liked me, and he did not like Charles. He came to me one night in Nanking, a few days before we were to start for Yunnan. He tried to dissuade me from the journey. He was a bit vague about reasons, talked of my condition, hard traveling and so on, but that was ridiculous. At last I asked him point-blank—why? Then he said that Charles was secretly meeting a Chinese captain, by name—Li-kong. I asked what of it, he had a right to pick his friends. Li-kong was suspected of being in touch with certain outlaws operating in Szechwan and Yunnan, and of receiving and disposing of the best of their booty. Li-kong: 'If both you and Martin die before the baby is born, Charles will inherit everything. He's next of kin and the only one, for you have nobody.' Kenwood said:

"You're going up into Yunnan. How easy to send word to one of these bands to look out for you. And then brother Charles would have it all. Of course, there's no use saying anything to your husband. He trusts everybody, and Charles most of all. All that would happen would be my dismissal.

"And of course that was true. But I couldn't believe Charles, for all he hated me so, would do this to Martin. There were two of us, and Kenwood and a nice Scotch woman I found at Nanking, a Miss Mackenzie, who agreed to come along to look after me in event of my needing it. There were twenty of us in all—the others Chinese boys, thoroughly good, thoroughly dependable. We came North slowly, unhurriedly. I said that Martin was a boy inside. No need to tell you again of his affection for you. And he loved China—the old China. He said it lived now only in a few places, and Yunnan was first. And he had it in his mind that our baby should be born— here—"

She sat silent, then laughed. "And so it will be. But not as Martin dreamed…" She was silent again. She said, as though faintly puzzled: "It was not—human—to laugh at that!" She went on serenely: "We came on and on slowly. Sampans on the rivers, and I by litter mostly. Always easily, easily…because of the baby. Then two weeks ago Kenwood told me that he had word we were to be attacked at a certain place. He had been years in China, knew how to get information and I knew he had watched and cajoled and threatened and bribed ever since we had entered the hills. He said he, had arranged a counter-attack that would catch the trappers in their own trap. He cursed Charles dreadfully, saying he was behind it. He said that if we could only get to Yu Ch'ien we would be safe. Afterwards he told me that he must have been sold wrong information. The counter-attack had drawn blank. I told him he was letting his imagination run away with him.

"We went on. Then came the ambush. It wasn't a matter of ransom. It was a matter of wiping us out.

"They gave us no chance. So it must have been that we were worth more to them dead than alive. That realization came to me as I stood at the door of my tent and saw Martin cut down, poor Mackenzie fall. Kenwood could have escaped as I did—but he died to give me time to get away..."

"Yu Ch'ien, what have you done to me?" asked Jean Meredith, dreamily. "I have seen my husband butchered...I have seen a man give up his life for me...and still I feel no more emotion than as though they had been reeds under the sickle...what have you done to me, Yu Ch'ien?"

He answered: "Daughter—when you are dead, and all those now living are dead—will it matter?"

She answered, shaking her head: "But—I am not dead! Nor are those now living dead. And I should rather be human, Yu Ch'ien. And suffer," He said: "It may not be, my daughter." "I wish I could feel," she said. "Good God, but I wish I could feel..."

She said: "That is all. Kenwood threw himself in front of me. I ran. I came to wide steps. I climbed them—up and up. I saw a fox—I saw a woman where I had seen the fox—"

He said: "You saw a Tibetan, a half-caste, who threw himself upon those who followed you, howling like a mad dog. You saw that Tibetan cut down by the knives of his men. I came with my men before he died. We brought him here. I searched his dying mind. He told me that they had been hired to wipe out your party by a Shensi leader of hung-hutzes. And that he had been promised not only the loot of your party if all were slain, but a thousand taels besides. And that when he asked who guaranteed this sum, this leader, in his cups, had told him the Captain Li-kong."

She cupped her chin in hand, looked out over the blue pool to the pagoda. She said at last: "So Kenwood was right! And I am right. It was Charles..."

She said: "I feel a little, Yu Ch'ien. But what I feel is not pleasant. It is hate, Yu Ch'ien..."

She said: "I am only twenty-four. It is rather young to die, Yu Ch'ien, isn't it? But then—what was it your woman's voice said while I was in the darkness? That the self of mine whom I would pity died when Martin did? She was right, Yu Ch'ien—or you were. And I think I will not be sorry to join that other self."

The sun was sinking. An amethyst veil dropped over the conical mountains. Suddenly they seemed to flatten, to become transparent. The whole valley between the peaks grew luminously crystalline. The blue pagoda shone as though made of dark sapphires behind which little suns burned. She sighed: "It is very beautiful, Yu Ch'ien. I am glad to be here—until I die."

There was a patter of feet beside her. A fox came trotting down one of the carven runways. It looked up at her fearlessly with glowing green eyes. Another slipped from the cover of the pool and another and another. They lapped the blue water fearlessly, eyes glinting swift side-glances at her, curiously...

The days slipped by her, the weeks — a month. Each day she sat in the seat of the foxes beside the pool, watching the willows trail their tendrils, the lilies like great rosy pearls open and close and die and be reborn on the pool's blue breast; watching the crystalline green dusks ensorcell the conical peaks, and watching the foxes that came when these dusks fell.

They were friendly now, the foxes — knew her, sat beside her, studying her; but never did she see the lithe fox with the lock of white between its slanting green eyes. She grew to know the brown woman Fienwi and the sturdy servitors. And from the scattered villages pilgrims came to the shrine; they looked at her fearfully, shyly; as she sat on the seat of the foxes, prostrating themselves before her as though she were some spirit to be placated by worship.

And each day was as the day before, and she thought: Without sorrow, without fear, without gladness, without hope there is no difference between the days, and therefore what difference does it make if I die tomorrow or a year hence?

Whatever the anodyne that steeped her soul — whether from vague woman of the steps or from Yu Ch'ien — it had left her with no emotion. Except that she knew she must bear it, she had no feeling even toward her unborn baby. Once, indeed, she had felt a faint curiosity. That this wise priest of the Foxes' Temple had his own means of learning what he desired of the outer world, she was well aware.

She said: "Does Charles know as yet of the ambush— know that I am still alive?"

He answered: "Not yet. The messengers who were sent to Li-kong did not reach him. It will be weeks before he knows."

She said: "And then he will come here. Will the baby be born when he comes, Yu Ch'ien?"

He answered: "Yes."

"And shall I be alive, Yu Ch'ien?"

He did not answer. She laughed.

It was one twilight, in the middle of the Hour of the Dog, that she turned to him, sitting in the garden beside the pool.

"My time has come, Yu Ch'ien. The child stirs."

They carried her into the temple. She lay upon the bed, while the brown woman stooped over her, ministering to her, helping her. The only light in the temple chamber came from five ancient lanterns of milky jade through whose thin sides the candles gleamed, turning them into five small moons. She felt little pain. She thought: I owe that to Yu Ch'ien, I suppose. And the minutes fled by until it was the Hour of the Boar.

She heard a scratching at the temple door. The priest opened it. He spoke softly, one word, a word often on his lips, and she knew it meant "patience." She could see through the opened door into the garden. There were small globular green lights all about, dozens of them, like gnome lanterns.

She said drowsily: "My little foxes wait. Let them enter, Yu Ch'ien."

"Not yet, my daughter."

The Hour of the Boar passed. Midnight passed. There was a great silence in the temple. It seemed to her that all the temple was waiting, that even the unfaltering light of the five small moons on the altar was waiting. She thought: Even the child is waiting...and for what?

And suddenly a swift agony shook her and she cried out. The brown woman held tight her hands that tried to beat the air. The priest called, and into the room came four of the sturdy servants of the temple. They carried large vessels in which was water steaming hot and water which did not steam and so, she reasoned idly, must be cold. They kept their backs to her, eyes averted.

The priest touched her eyes, stroked her flanks, and the agony was gone as swiftly as it had come. She watched the servants pour the waters into the ancient Tang font and slip away, backs still turned to her, faces averted.

She had not seen the door open, but there was a fox in the room. It was ghostly in the dim light of the jade lamps, yet she could see it stepping daintily toward her...a vixen, lithe and graceful as a woman...with slanted eyes, sea-green, brilliant as jewels...the fox of the steps whom she had called sister...

And now she was looking up into a woman's face. An exquisite face with sea-green, slanted eyes under a broad ' brow, whose hair of russet-red came to a small peak in the center of that brow, and above the peak a lock of silvery white...the eyes gazed into hers, and although they caressed her, there was in them a faint mockery, a delicate malice.

The woman was naked. Although Jean Meredith could not wrest her own eyes from the slanting green ones, she could see the curve of delicate shoulders, the rounded breasts, the slender hips. It was as though the woman stood poised upon her own breasts, without weight, upon airy feet. There was a curious tingling coolness in her breasts...more pleasant than warmth... and it was as though the woman were sinking into her, becoming a part of her. The face came nearer...nearer...the eyes were now close to hers, and mockery and malice gone from them...in them was only gentleness and promise...she felt cool lips touch hers...

The face was gone. She was sinking, sinking, unresistingly...gratefully...through a luminous greyness ...then into a soft blind darkness...she was being cradled by it, sinking ever deeper and deeper. She cried out once, as though frightened: Martin! Then she cried again, voice vibrant with joy: Martin!

One of the five moon lamps upon the jade altar darkened. Went out.

The brown woman was prostrate upon her face beside the bed. The priest touched her with his foot. He said: "Prepare. Be swift." She bent over the still body.

There was a movement beside the altar. Four foxes stepped daintily from its shadows toward the Tang front. They were vixens, and they came like graceful women, and the coat of each was silken russet-red, their eyes brilliant, sea-green and slanting, and upon each forehead was a lock of silvery white. They drew near the brown woman, watching her.

The priest walked to the doors and threw them open. Into the temple slipped fox after fox...a score, two score...the temple filled with them. They ringed the ancient font, squatting, red tongues lolling, eyes upon the bed.

The priest walked to the bed. In his hand was a curiously shaped, slender knife of bronze, double-edged, sharp as a surgeon's knife. The brown woman threw herself again upon the floor. The priest leaned over the bed, began with a surgeon's deftness and delicacy to cut. The four vixens drew close, watching every movement—-

Suddenly there wailed through the temple the querulous crying of a new-born child.

The priest walked from the bed toward the font...He held the child in his hands, and hands and child were red with blood. The vixens walked beside him. The foxes made way for them, closing their circles as they passed. The four vixens halted, one at each of the font's four sides. They did not sit. They stood with gaze fastened upon the priest.

The priest ringed the font, bending before each of the four vixens, holding out the child until each had touched it with her tongue. He lifted the child by the feet, held it dangling head down, high above his head, turning so that all the other foxes could see it.

He plunged it five times into the water of the font.

As abruptly as the first moon lantern had gone out, so darkened the other four.

There was a rustling, the soft patter of many pads. Then silence.

Yu Ch'ien called. There was the gleam of lanterns borne by the servants. The brown woman raised herself from the floor. He placed the child in her hands. He said: "It is finished — and it is begun. Care for her."

Thus was born the daughter of Jean and Martin Meredith in the ancient Temple of the Foxes. Born in the heart of the Hour of the Fox, so called in those parts of China where the ancient beliefs still live because it is at the opposite pole of the Hour of the Horse, which animal at certain times and at certain places, has a magic against which the magic of the Fox may not prevail.

CHAPTER III

THE HOME OF HEAVENLY ANTICIPATIONS honored with its presence Peking, not yet at that time renamed Peiping. It was hidden in the heart of the Old City. The anticipations discussed there were usually the reverse of heavenly—or, if not, then dealing with highly unorthodox realms of beatitude.

But except for its patrons none ever knew what went on within its walls. There was never any leakage of secrets through those walls. Peculiarly ultimate information could be obtained at the Home of Heavenly Anticipations—so long as it did not pertain to its patrons.

It was, in fact, a clearing house for enterprises looked upon with a certain amount of disfavor even by many uncivilized countries: enterprises such as blackmail, larceny on the grand scale, smuggling, escapes, piracies, removal of obstacles by assassination and so on. Its abbots collected rich tithes from each successful operation in return for absolute protection from interruption, eavesdropping and spies, and for the expert and thoroughly trustworthy advices upon any point of any enterprise which needed to be cleared up before action.

Prospective members of the most exclusive of London's clubs were never scanned with such completeness as were applicants for the right to enter the Home of Heavenly Anticipations—and one had to be a rather complete scoundrel to win that right. But to those who sought such benefits as it offered, they were worth all the difficulty in securing them.

Charles Meredith sat in one of its rooms, three weeks to a night from the birth of Jean Meredith's baby. He was not a member, but it was the privilege of accredited patrons to entertain guests to whom secrecy was as desirable as to themselves — or who might prove refractory.

It was a doubtful privilege for these guests, although they were not aware of it, because it was always quite possible that they might never appear again in their usual haunts. In such event it was almost impossible to trace them back to the Home of Heavenly Anticipations. Always, on their way to it, they had been directed to leave their vehicle, coolie-carriage or what not at a certain point and to wait until another picked them up. Beyond that point they were never traced. Or if their bodies were later found, it was always under such circumstances that no one could point a finger at the Home of Heavenly Anticipations, which was as expert on alibis for corpses as for crooks.

Although he knew nothing of this, Charles Meredith was uneasy. For one thing, he had a considerable sum of money in his pocket—a very considerable sum. To be explicit, fifty thousand dollars. For another thing, he had not the slightest idea of where he was.

He had dismissed his hotel coolie at a designated point, had been approached by another who gave the proper word of recognition, had been whisked through street after street, then through a narrow alley, then through a door opening into a winding passage, thence into a plain reception hall where a bowing Chinese had met him and led him to the room. He had seen no one, and he heard no

sound. Under the circumstances, he appreciated privacy —
but damn it, there was a limit! And where was Li-kong?

He got up and walked about nervously. It gave him
some satisfaction to feel the automatic holstered under his
left arm-pit. He was tall, rather rangy and his shoulders
stooped a little. He had clear eyes whose grey stood out a
bit startlingly from his dark face; a good forehead, a
somewhat predatory beaked nose; his worst feature, his
mouth, which hinted self-indulgence and cruelty.
Seemingly an alert, capable American man of affairs, not at
all one who would connive at the murder of his own
brother.

He turned at the opening of the door. Li-kong came in.
Li-kong was a graduate of an American college. His father
had cherished hopes of a high diplomatic career, with his
American training as part of its foundation. He had repaid
it by learning in exhaustive detail the worst of American
life. This, grafted to his natural qualifications, had given
him high place in the Home of Heavenly Anticipations
and among its patrons.

He was in the most formal of English evening dress,
looked completely the person his father had hoped he
would be instead of what he actually was — without
principles, morals, mercy or compunction whatever.

Meredith's nervousness found vent in an irritable,
"You've been a hell of a long time getting here, Li-kong!"

The eyes of the Chinese flickered, but he answered urbanely: "Bad news flies fast. Good news is slow. I am neither early nor late."

Meredith asked suspiciously: "What the hell do you mean by that?"

Li-kong said, eyes watchful: "Your honorable elder brother has ascended the dragon."

Meredith's grey eyes glittered. The cruelty stood out on his mouth, unmasked. Li-kong said before he could speak: "All with him, even his unworthy servants, ascended at the same time. All except—" He paused.

Meredith's body tightened, his head thrust forward. He asked in a thin voice: "Except?"

The eyes of the Chinese never left him. He said:

"When you rebuked me a moment ago for slowness, I answered that I was neither early nor late. I must therefore bear good news and bad—"

The American interrupted: "Damn you, Li-kong, who got away?"

The Chinese answered: "Your brother's wife."

Meredith's face whitened, then blackened with fury. He whispered: "Christ!"

He roared: "So you bungled it!" His hand twitched up to the gun under his arm-pit, then dropped. He asked: "Where is she?"

The Chinese must have seen that betraying movement, but he gave no sign. He answered: "She fled to the Temple of the Foxes—to your brother's old friend, the priest Yu Ch'ien."

The other snarled: "What were your bunglers about, to let her go? Why didn't they go after her?"

"They did go after her! Of what happened thereafter, you shall hear—when you have paid me my money, my friend."

"Paid you!" Meredith's fury mastered him at this. "With the bitch alive? I'll see you in hell before you get a cent from me."

The Chinese said calmly: "But since then she has also ascended the dragon in the footsteps of her lord. She died in childbirth."

"They both are dead—" Meredith sank into the chair, trembling like one from whom tremendous strain has lifted. "Both dead—"

The Chinese watched him, malicious anticipation in his eyes. "But the child—lived!" he said.

For a long minute the American sat motionless, looking at him. And now he did not lose control. He said coldly: "So you have been playing with me, have you? Well, now listen to me — you get nothing until the child has followed its father and mother. Nothing! And if it is in your mind to blackmail me, remember you can bring no charge against me without sending yourself to the executioner. Think over that, you leering yellow ape!"

The Chinese lighted a cigarette. He said mildly:

"Your brother is dead, according to plan. His wife is dead through that same plan, even though she did not die when the others did. There was nothing in the bargain concerning the child. And I do not think you could reach the child without me." He smiled. "Is it not said, of two brothers, he who thinks himself the invulnerable one — that is the fool?"

Meredith said nothing, eyes bleak on him. Li-kong went on: "Also, I have information to impart, advice to give — necessary to you if you determine to go for the child. As you must — if you want her. And finally — is it not written in the Yih King, the Book of Changes, that a man's mind should have many entrances but only one exit! In this house the saying is reversed. It has only one entrance but many exits — and the door-keeper of each one of them is death."

Again he paused, then said: "Think over that, you welching white brother-killer!"

The American quivered. He sprang up, reaching for his gun. Strong hands grasped his elbows, held him helpless. Li-kong sauntered to him, drew out the automatic, thrust it into his own pocket. The hands released Meredith. He looked behind him. Two Chinese stood there. One held a crimson bow-string, the other a double-edged short-sword.

"Two of the deaths that guard the exits." Li-kong's voice was courtesy itself. "You may have your choice. I recommend the sword — it is swifter."

Ruthless Meredith was, and no coward, but he recognized here a ruthlessness complete as his own. "You win," he said. "I'll pay."

"And now," smiled Li-kong.

Meredith drew out the bundle of notes and passed them to him. The Chinese counted them and nodded. He spoke to the two executioners and they withdrew. He said very seriously: "My friend, it is well for you I recognize that insults by a younger people have not the same force that they would have if spoken by one of my own race, so much older than yours. In the Yih King it is written that we must not be confused by similitude, that the superior man places not the same value upon the words of a child as he does upon those of a grown man, although the words be identical. It is well also for you that I feel a certain obligation. Not personally, but because an unconsidered factor has caused a seed sown in this house to bring forth a deformed blossom. It is," continued Li-kong, still very seriously, "a reflection upon its honor —"

He smiled at that, and said, "Or rather, its efficiency. I suggest, therefore, that we discuss the matter without heat or further recrimination of any kind."

Meredith said: "I am sorry I said what I did, Li-kong. It was childish temper. I apologize."

The Chinese bowed, but he did not take the hand the other extended. Nor did he recall his own words.

He said: "The child is at the Temple of the Foxes. In Kansu, it is an extremely sacred shrine. She is in charge of Yu Ch'ien, who is not only wise but powerful, and in addition was your honorable late brother's devoted friend. If Yu Ch'ien suspects, then you will have great difficulty in adding to your brother's and your sister-in-law's happiness in Heaven by restoring to them their daughter. You may assume that Yu Ch'ien does suspect—and knows."

Meredith asked incredulously: "Why should he suspect? How could he know?"

Li-kong tapped his cigarette thoughtfully before he answered: "The priest is very wise. Also, like myself, he has had the advantage of contact with your admirable civilization. The woman was with him for weeks, and so he must know who would benefit by the—ah, expungement of your revered relatives. He might think it highly suspicious that those responsible for the regrettable affair did not pursue the custom of holding the principals for ransom instead of—ah, expunging them on the spot. Naturally, he would ask himself why. Finally, Yu Ch'ien is locally reported to have sources of information not open to other men—I mean living men. The dead," observed Li-kong sardonically, "of course know everything."

Meredith said contemptuously: "What do you mean? Spiritism, divination—that rot?"

Li-kong considered pensively, answered at last: "No—not exactly that. Something closer, rather to the classical idea of communion with elemental intelligences, nature spirits, creatures surviving from an older world than man's—but still of earth. Something like the spirits that answered from the oaks of Dodona, or that spoke to the Sybyl in the grotto of Cumæ, or in more modern times appeared in, and instructed Joan of Arc from, the branches of the arbre fee, the fairy tree of Domremy."

Meredith laughed. "Good God! And this—from you!"

Li-kong said imperturbably: "This from me! I am—what I am. I believe in nothing. Yet I tell you that I would not go up those steps to the Temple of the ' for all the gold you could give me. Not—now!"

Meredith thought: He is trying to frighten me. The yellow dog is trying to keep me from the temple. Why? He spoke only the last word of the thought: "Why?"

The Chinese answered: "China is old. The ancient beliefs are still strong. There are, for example, the legends of the fox women. The fox women are nature spirits. Intelligences earthy but not human—akin to those in Dodona's oaks, Cumæ's grotto, Joan of Arc's fairy tree. Believed in—especially in Kansu. These—let us say spirits—have certain powers far exceeding the human. Bear with me while I tell you of a few of these powers. They can assume two earthly shapes only—that of a fox and that of a beautiful woman. There are fox men, too, but the weight of the legends are upon the women. Since for them time does not exist, they are mistresses of time. To those who come under their power, they can cause a day to seem like a thousand years, or a thousand years like a day. They can open the doors to other worlds—worlds of terror, worlds of delight. If such worlds are illusions, they do not seem so to those for whom they are opened. The fox women can make or mar journeys."

Meredith thought: Come, now we're getting down to it.

The Chinese went quietly on: "They can create other illusions. Phantoms, perhaps—but if so, phantoms whose blows maim or kill. They are capricious, bestowing good fortune or ill regardless of the virtue or the lack of it of the recipient. They are peculiarly favorable to women with child. They can, by invitation, enter a woman, passing through her breasts or beneath her finger nails. They can enter an unborn child, or rather a child about to be born. In such cases, the mother dies—nor is the manner of birth the normal one. They cannot oust the soul of the child, but they can dwell beside it, influencing it. Quaint fancies, my friend, in none of which I have belief. Yet because of them nothing could induce me to climb the steps to the Temple of the Foxes."

Meredith thought: He's trying to frighten me away! What the hell does he think I am—to be frightened by such superstitious drivel? He said, in that thin voice with which he spoke when temper was mastering him:

"What's your game, Li-kong? Another double-cross? You're trying to tell me that if I were you, I wouldn't go to the temple for the brat. Why?"

The Chinese said: "My friend, I have played the game with you. I do not say that if I were you, I would not go. I say that if you were I, you would not. A quite different thing."

The other swung clenched fist down upon the table. "Don't tell me you expect me to take seriously that farrago of nonsense! You don't expect me to give up now because of a yellow —" He checked himself abruptly.

The Chinese completed the sentence politely: "Because of a yellow man's superstition! No, but let me point out a few rather disquieting things. The Temple of the Foxes is believed to be the home of five of these fox women. Five — spirits — who are sisters. Three messengers were sent me with the news of the ambush. The first should have reached me within three weeks after it happened. He has vanished. The second was despatched with other news a week later. He too vanished. But the third, bearing the news of the death of your brother's wife, the birth of the child, came as on the wings of the wind. Why the failure of the first two? Because someone desired to keep you in ignorance until after that birth? Who?

"Again, no word has come from Kansu, except by this messenger, of the attack on your brother's party. This, my friend, places you in a dilemma. You cannot betray your knowledge of his death without subjecting yourself to questioning as to how that knowledge came to you. You cannot, therefore, send for the child. You must yourself go—upon some pretext. I think that whoever sped the third messenger on his way intends that you shall go—yourself. Why?"

Meredith struck the table again. "I'll go!"

"Third," continued Li-kong, "my messenger said that the woman who fled ran up the steps of the Temple of the Foxes. And that when they were almost upon her—a fox stood between her and them. And that fox changed into a woman who changed their leader into a mad dog. At which—they ran. So I think," said Li-kong meditatively, "would I have run!"

Meredith said nothing, but his hand beat steadily on the table and the grey eyes were furious.

"You are thinking," said the Chinese, "'The yellow dogs! Of course they would run! Filled with rum or opium! Of course!'"

It was precisely what he had been thinking, but Meredith made no answer.

"And finally," said Li-kong, "your brother's wife died when the child was born—"

"Because, I suppose, the fox bitch crawled into her!" jeered Meredith, and leaning back, whined thin, high-pitched laughter.

The Chinese lost for a moment his calm, half arose, then dropped back. He said patiently: "If you go up the steps — ride a horse. Preferably an English horse that has hunted foxes."

He lighted another cigarette. "But that is superstition. Nevertheless, if you go, take two men with you as free from taint — as you are. I know two such men. One is a German, the other French. Bold men and hard men. Travel alone, the three of you, as far as you can. At all times keep as few Chinese with you as possible. When you go to the temple, go up the steps alone. Take no Chinese with you there." He said gravely: "I vouch for these two men. Better still, the Home of Heavenly Anticipations vouches for them. They will want money, of course."

Meredith asked: "How much?"

"I don't know. They're not cheap. Probably five thousand dollars at most."

Meredith thought: Here's what he's been leading up to. It's a trap!

Again it was as though Li-kong had read his thoughts. He said very deliberately: "Meredith, listen to me! I want nothing more from you nor through you. I have not spoken to these men. They do not know, nor will they know from me, anything of that transaction for which you have just paid. I am through with it. I am through with you! I do not like you. I hope never to see you again. Is that plain American talk?"

Meredith said, as deliberately: "I like it. Go on."

"All that they need know is that you are anxious about your brother. When in due time during your journey you discover that he and his wife are dead, and that there is a child, you will naturally want to bring that child back with you. If you are denied the child, and killing is necessary, they will kill. That is all. I will put you in touch with these two men. And I will see to it that none with whom I have relations embarrass you on your way to Kansu, nor on your way back—if you come back. Except for that obligation of which I have spoken, I would not do even this. I would not lift a finger to help you. After you leave this house, you shall be to me as though you never had been. I want nothing to do with Yu Ch'ien and those who go to the Temple of the Foxes. If we should meet again— never speak to me! Do not show you have known me! Never speak to me, never write to me, do not think of me. I am through with you! Is that clear?"

Meredith nodded, smiling. He thought: I was wrong about him wanting to keep me from the place. The yellow rat is frightened...he believes in his own bogies! America and everything else couldn't knock the superstition out of him!

The thought amused him. It gave him a contemptuous tolerance of Li-kong, a pleasant knowledge of superiority. He said, not bothering to keep the contempt from his voice: "Clearer than you know, Li-kong. Where do I meet your friends?"

"They can be at your hotel at one, if it suits you."

"It suits me. Their names?"

"They will tell you. They will bear credentials from me."

Li-kong arose. He stood beside the door, bowing courteously. Meredith passed through. They went along another passage and through a winding alley out into a street. It was not the same street from which he had entered. Nor did he recognize it. A coolie-car waited. Li-kong bowed him into it.

"May our shadows never touch again," said Li-kong ceremoniously. He added, for the first time menacingly: "For your health."

He turned and passed into the alley. The coolie broke into a swift trot, and away.

CHAPTER IV

IT WAS MID-AFTERNOON a month later that he rode out of the green glen and looked up the first steep flight of the ancient steps to the Temple of the Foxes. Riding beside him were von Brenner and Lascelles, the two bold and hard men Li-kong had recommended. They were all of that, but they were also discreet men. They had accepted without comment his explanation of seeking news of his brother, had been properly sympathetic and had asked him no embarrassing questions. Both could speak the Mandarin as well as several of the dialects. Lascelles knew Kansu, was even familiar with the locality in which was the Temple of the Foxes.

Meredith had thought it wise to make inquiries at various places through which he knew Martin had passed, and here the German and the Frenchman acted as his interpreters. When they reported that at these points his brother's party had been in excellent health, they did so with every outward evidence of belief that such tidings were welcome to him.

Either they were excellent actors or Li-kong had kept faith with him and told them nothing beyond what had been agreed. Confidence in the second possibility however had been somewhat disturbed shortly after entering Kansu. The Frenchman had said he thought, somewhat too casually, that if it was desirable to get to the temple without passing through any village within a day's march, he knew a way. He added that while undoubtedly the temple's priest would know they were coming, he would expect them to follow the usual route. Therefore, he could possibly be taken by surprise.

Meredith smelled a trap. To accept the suggestion was to admit that the temple had been the real object of his journey, the reason he had given a subterfuge, and the anxious inquiries he had made along the line of march a blind. He answered sharply that there was no reason for any surprise visit, that the priest Yu Ch'ien, a venerable scholar, was an old friend of his brother, and that if the party had reached him there was no further cause for anxiety. Why did Lascelles think he desired any secrecy in his search? The Frenchman replied politely that if he had known of such friendship the thought would not have occurred to him, of course.

As a matter of fact, Meredith felt no more fear of Yu Ch'ien than he did of Li-kong's fox woman. Whenever he thought of how the Chinese had tried to impress him with that yellow Mother Goose yarn, he felt a contemptuous amusement that more than compensated him for the humiliation of having been forced to pay the blood money. He had often listened to Martin extol Yu Ch'ien's wisdom and virtues, but that only proved what a complete impractical ass Martin had been...gone senile prematurely, in brain at least...that was plain enough when he married that gold-digger young enough to be his daughter...no longer the brother he had known...who could tell what he might have done next...some senility which would have brought ruin to them all...a senile crazy brain in Martin's still sound body, that was all...if Martin had been suffering from some agonizing and incurable disease and had asked him to put him out of his misery, he would certainly have done so...well, what was the difference between that and what he had done? That the girl and her brat should also have to suffer was too bad...but it had been made necessary by Martin's own senility.

Thus he justified himself. At the same time there was no reason why he should take these two men into his confidence.

What he should do with the brat when he had it was not quite clear. It was only two months old—and it was a long journey back to Peking. There must be some woman taking care of it at the temple. He would arrange that she go with them to Peking. If some accident happened, or if the child caught something or other on the way back—that

71

would not be his fault. Her proper place, obviously, was with her father's family. Not in a heathen temple back of nowhere in China. Nobody could blame him for wanting to bring her back…even if anything did happen to her.

But on second thought, not so good. He would have to take back proof that this child was theirs. Proof of birth. It would be better to bring her alive to Peking…even better, it might be, if it lived until he had taken it back to the States and the whole matter of trusteeship and guardianship had been legally adjusted. There was plenty of time. And he would have his half-million, and the increased percentage from the estate to tide him over the gap between now and until—something happened, and the whole estate would be his. He thought callously: Well, the brat is insured as far as Peking at any rate.

They had passed through a village that morning. The headman had met them, and in answer to the usual questioning, had given a complete account of the massacre, of Jean's escape, of her death later at the temple and of the child's birth. It was so complete, even to the dates, that he felt a stirring of faint suspicion. It was a little as though the story had been drilled into this man. And now and then he would call this one or that among the villagers for corroboration. But Charles had shown the proper shades of grief, and desire to punish the killers. And Brenner and Lascelles had exerted themselves to comfort him in orthodox fashion.

He had said at last: "The first thing to do is get the baby safely back to Peking. I can get capable white nurses there. I'll have to find a woman here to look after it until we reach Peking. I want to get the child to the States and in my wife's care as soon as I can. And I want to start the machinery going to punish my brother's murderers — although I realize that's a forlorn hope."

They had agreed with him that it was most desirable to get the child to his wife in quickest possible time, and that hope of punishing the killers was indeed a forlorn one.

And now he stood looking up the ancient steps at whose end was the child. He said: "You couldn't ride a horse up that, unless it was a circus horse. And these are not."

Lascelles smiled. "It is impossible to ride to the temple. There are steeper flights than this. And there is no trail or other road. We must walk."

Meredith said suspiciously: "You seem to know a lot about this place, Lascelles. Ever been to the temple?"

The Frenchman answered: "No, but I have talked to those who have."

Meredith grinned. "Li-kong told me to take a horse. He said the fox women were afraid of it."

Brenner laughed. "Die Fuchs-Damen! I haf always wanted to see one. Joost as I always wanted to see one of those bowmen of Mons they haf spoken so highly of in the War. Yah! I would like to try a bullet on the bowmen, but I would haf other treatment for the fox women. Yah!"

Lascelles said noncommittally: "It's hard to get some things out of the mind of a Chinese."

Brenner said to Meredith: "There is one question I haf to ask. How far iss it that we go in getting this child? Suppose this priest thinks it better you do not haf it? How far iss it that we go to persuade him, hein?" He added meditatively: "The headman said that there are with the priest three women and four men." He said even more meditatively: "The headsman he was very full of detail. Yah—he knew a lot. I do not like that—quite."

Lascelles nodded, saying nothing, looking at Meredith interrogatively.

Meredith said: "I do not see for what reason or upon what grounds Yu Ch'ien can deny me the child. I am its uncle, its natural guardian. Its father, my brother so designated me in the event of his death. Well, he is dead. If the priest refuses to give it up peaceably I would certainly be justified in using force to secure it. If the priest were hurt—we would not be to blame. If his men attacked us and were hurt—we would be blameless. One way or another—I take the child."

Lascelles said somewhat grimly: "If it comes to fighting, we ride back along that way I told you of. We will go through no village within a day's journey from here. It will not be healthy for us in Kansu—the speed at which we must go will not be healthy for the child."

Meredith said: "I am sure we'll have no trouble with Yu Ch'ien."

They had brought a fourth horse with them, a sturdy beast with wide Chinese saddle such as a woman rides. They tethered the four horses and began to mount the steps. At first they talked, then their voices seemed to be absorbed in the silence, to grow thin. They stopped talking.

The tall pines watched them as they passed—the crouching shrubs watched them. They saw no one, heard nothing—but gradually they became as watchful as the pines and bushes, alert, hands gripping the butts of their pistols as though the touch gave them confidence. They came over the brow of the hill and the sweat was streaming from them as it streams from horses frightened by something they sense but can neither see nor hear.

It was as though they had passed out of some peril-haunted jungle into safety. They still said nothing to each other, but they straightened, drew deep breaths, and their hands fell from their pistols. They looked down upon the peacock-tiled roof of the Temple of the Foxes and upon its blue pool of peace. A man sat beside it on a stone seat. As they watched him, he arose and walked toward the temple. At each side of him went a pair of what seemed russet-red dogs. Suddenly they saw that these were not dogs, but foxes.

They came down over the brow of the hill to the rear of the temple. In its brown stone there was no door, only six high windows that seemed to watch them come. They saw no one. They skirted the temple and reached its front. The man they had seen at the pool stood there, as though awaiting them. The foxes were gone.

75

The three halted as one, involuntarily. Meredith had expected to see an old, old man—gentle, a little feeble, perhaps. The face he saw was old, no doubt of that—but the eyes were young and prodigiously alive. Large and black and liquid, they held his. He was clothed in a symboled robe of silvery blue on whose breast in silver was a fox's head.

Meredith thought: What if he isn't what I expected! He shook his head impatiently, as though to get rid of some numbness. He stepped forward, hand outstretched. He said: "I am Charles Meredith. You are Yu Ch'ien—my brother's friend—"

The priest said: "I have been expecting you, Charles Meredith. You already know what happened. The village headman mercifully took from me the burden of delivering to you the first blossom of sorrowful knowledge."

Meredith thought: How the devil did he know that?

The village is half a day away. We came swiftly, and no runner could have reached here before us.

The priest had taken his outstretched hand. He did not clasp it palm to palm, but held it across the top, thumb pressed to wrist. Meredith felt a curious tingling coolness dart from wrist to shoulder. The black eyes were looking deep into his, and he felt the same tingling coolness in his brain. His hand was released, the gaze withdrawn. He felt as though something had been withdrawn from his mind with it.

76

"And your friends—" Yu Ch'ien grasped von Brenner's hand in the same way, black eyes searching the German's. He turned to Lascelles. The French thrust his hands behind him, avoided the eyes. He bowed and said: "For me, it is too great honor, venerable father of wisdom."

For an instant Yu Ch'ien's gaze rested on him thoughtfully. He spoke to Meredith: "Of your brother and your brother's wife there is nothing more to be said. They have passed. You shall see the child."

Meredith answered bluntly: "I came to take her with me, Yu Ch'ien."

The priest said as though he had not heard: "Come into the temple and you shall see her."

He walked through the time-bitten pillars into the room where Jean Meredith had died. They followed him. It was oddly dark within the temple '. Meredith supposed that it was the transition from the sunny brightness. It was as though the chamber was filled with silent, watchful brown shadows. There was an altar of green stone on which were five ancient lamps of milky jade. They were circular, and in four of them candles burned, turning them into four small moons. The priest led them toward this altar. Not far from the altar was an immense vessel of bronze, like a baptismal font. Between altar and vessel was an old Chinese cradle, and nestled in its cushions was a baby. It was a girl child, fast asleep, one little dimpled fist doubled up to its mouth. The priest walked to the opposite side of the cradle.

He said softly: "Your brother's daughter, Charles Meredith. Bend over. I desire to show you something, let your friends look too."

The three bent over the cradle. The priest gently opened the child's swathings. Upon its breast, over its heart, was a small scarlet birth-mark shaped like a candle flame wavering in the wind. Lascelles lifted his hand, finger pointing, but before he could speak, the priest had caught his wrist. He looked into the Frenchman's eyes. He said sternly: "Do not waken her."

The Frenchman stared at him for a moment, then said through stiff lips: "You devil!"

The priest dropped his wrist. He said to Meredith, tranquilly: "I show you the birth-mark so you may know the child when you see her again. It will be long, Charles Meredith, before you do see her again."

A quick rage swept Meredith but before he succumbed to it he found time to wonder at its fury. He whispered: "Cover him, von Brenner! Throttle him, Lascelles!"

He bent down to lift the baby from the cradle. He stiffened, hands clutching at empty air. The baby and cradle were gone. He looked up. The priest was gone.

Where Yu Ch'ien had stood was a row of archers, a dozen of them. The light from the four lanterns shone shadedly upon them. They were in archaic mail, black lacquered helmets on their heads; under their visors yellow slanted eyes gleamed from impassive faces. Their bows were stretched, strings ready to loose, the triangular arrow heads at point like snakes poised to spring. He looked at them stupidly. Where had they come from? At the head of the line was a giant all of seven feet tall, old, with a face as though made of gnarled pear-wood. It was his arrow that pointed to Meredith's heart. The others — -

He sprang back — back between von Brenner and Lascelles. They stood, glaring unbelievingly as he had at that line of bowmen. He saw the German lift his pistol, heard him say thickly: "The bowmen of Mons —" heard Lascelles cry: "Drop it, you fool!" Heard the twang of a bow, the hiss of an arrow and saw an arrow pierce the German's wrist and saw the pistol fall to the temple floor.

Lascelles cried: "Don't move, Meredith!" The Frenchman's automatic rang upon the temple floor.

He heard a command — in the voice of Yu Ch'ien. The archers moved forward, not touching the three, but menacing them with their arrows. The three moved back.

Abruptly, beneath the altar, in the light of the four lanterns, he saw the cradle and the child within it, still asleep.

And beside the cradle, Yu Ch'ien.

The priest beckoned him. The line of archers opened as he walked forward. Yu Ch'ien looked at him with unfathomable eyes. He said in the same tranquil tones, utterly without anger or reproach:

"I know the truth. You think I could not prove that truth? You are right. I could not—in an earthly court. And you fear no other. But listen well—you have good reason to fear me! Some day your brother's child will be sent to you. Until she comes, look after her interests well and try in no manner directly or indirectly to injure her. You will have the money your brother left you. You will have your interest in her estate. You will have at least seven years before she comes. Use those years well, Charles Meredith—it is not impossible that you may build up much merit which will mitigate, even if it cannot cancel, your debt of wickedness. But this I tell you—do not try to regain this child before she is sent to you, nor attempt to molest her. After she comes to you—the matter is in other hands than mine. Do you understand me, Charles Meredith?"

He heard himself say: "I understand you. It shall be as you say."

Yu Ch'ien thrust his hand into his robe, drew out a package. He said: "Here are written the circumstances of your brother's death, his wife's death and the birth of the child. They are attested by me, and by witnesses of mine. I am well known far beyond the limits of this, my temple. My signature will be sufficient to prove the authenticity of the statements. I have given my reasons why I think it useless to attempt to bring the actual murderers of your brother and his party to justice. I have said that their leader was caught and executed. He was! My real reason for acting as I am may not be known by you. Now pick up those useless weapons of yours—useless at least here—take these papers and go!"

80

Meredith took the documents. He picked up the guns. He turned and walked stiffly through the bowmen to where von Brenner and Lascelles stood close to the temple doors, under the arrows of the bowmen. They mounted the hill and set their feet upon the ancient road.

Silent, like men half-awake, they passed through the lines of the watchful pines and at last into the glen where their horses stood tethered — -

There was an oath from the German. He was moving the wrist gingerly. And suddenly all three were like men who had just awakened. Von Brenner cried: "The arrow! I felt it — I saw it! But there iss no arrow and no mark. And my hand iss good as ever."

Lascelles said very quietly: "There was no arrow, von Brenner. There were no bowmen. Nevertheless, let us move from here quickly."

Meredith said: "But I saw the arrow strike. I saw the archers."

"When Yu Ch'ien gripped our wrists he gripped our minds," answered Lascelles. "If we had not believed in the reality of the bowmen — we would not have seen them. The arrow could not have hurt you, von Brenner. But the priest had trapped us. We had to believe in their reality." He untied his horse. He turned to Meredith, foot on stirrup: "Did Yu Ch'ien threaten you?"

Meredith answered with a touch of grim humor:

"Yes—but he gave me seven years for the threats to take effect."

Lascelles said: "Good. Then you and I, von Brenner, get back to Peking. We'll spend the night at that village of the too well informed headman—go back by the open road. But ride fast."

He gave the horse his knee and raced away. The other two followed. The horse with the wide Chinese saddle placidly watched them go.

Two hours after dusk they came to the village. The headman was courteous, provided them with food and shelter, but no longer was communicative. Meredith was quiet. Before they rolled into their blankets he said to Lascelles: "When the priest grasped your hand you were about to say something—something about that birth-mark on the child's breast. What was it?"

Lascelles said: "I was about to say that it was the symbol of the fox women."

Meredith said: "Don't tell me you believe in that damned nonsense!"

Lascelles answered: "I'm not telling you anything, except that the mark was the symbol of the fox women."

Von Brenner said: "I'fe seen some strange things in this damned China and elsewhere, Pierre. But neffer an arrow that pierced a man's wrist and hung there quivering—and then was gone. But the wrist dead—as mine wass."

Lascelles said: "Listen, Franz. This priest is a great man. What he did to us I have seen sorcerers, so-called, do to others in Tibet and in India. But never with such completeness, such clarity. The archers came from the mind of the priest into our minds—yes, that I know. But I tell you, Franz, that if you had believed that arrow had pierced your heart—your heart would not be alive as your wrist is! I tell you again—he is a great man, that priest."

Meredith said: "But—"

Lascelles said: "For Christ's sake, man, is it impossible for you to learn!" He rolled himself in his blankets. Went to sleep.

Meredith lay awake, thinking, for long. He thought;

Yu Ch'ien doesn't know a damned thing. If he did—why would he promise me the child? He knows he can't prove a thing. He thought: He thinks he can frighten me so that when the child comes of age she'll get what's coming to her...And he thought: Lascelles is as crazy as Li-kong. Those archers were hidden there all the time. They were real, all right. Or, if it was a matter of hypnotism, I'd like to see myself believe in them in New York! He laughed.

It was a damned good arrangement, he concluded. Probably the priest wouldn't send the brat back to him for ten years. But in the meantime—well, he'd like to see that file of archers in one of the Bronx night clubs! It was a good arrangement—for him. The priest was as senile as Martin...

THE WOMEN OF THE WOOD

MCKAY SAT ON THE BALCONY of the little inn that squatted like a brown gnome among the pines on the eastern shore of the lake.

It was a small and lonely lake high up in the Vosges; and yet, lonely is not just the word with which to tag its spirit; rather was it aloof, withdrawn. The mountains came down on every side, making a great tree-lined bowl that seemed, when McKay first saw it, to be filled with the still wine of peace.

McKay had worn the wings in the world war with honor, flying first with the French and later with his own country's forces. And as a bird loves the trees, so did McKay love them. To him they were not merely trunks and roots, branches and leaves; to him they were personalities. He was acutely aware of differences in character even among the same species—that pine was benevolent and jolly; that one austere and monkish; there stood a swaggering bravo, and there dwelt a sage wrapped in green meditation; that birch was a wanton— the birch near her was virginal, still a-dream.

The war had sapped him, nerve and brain and soul. Through all the years that had passed since then the wound had kept open. But now, as he slid his car down the vast green bowl, he felt its spirit reach out to him; reach out to him and caress and quiet him, promising him healing. He seemed to drift like a falling leaf through the clustered woods; to be cradled by gentle hands of the trees.

He had stopped at the little gnome of an inn, and there he had lingered, day after day, week after week.

The trees had nursed him; soft whisperings of leaves, slow chant of the needled pines, had first deadened, then driven from him the re-echoing clamor of the war and its sorrow. The open wound of his spirit had closed under their green healing; had closed and become scar; and even the scar had been covered and buried, as the scars on Earth's breast are covered and buried beneath the falling leaves of Autumn. The trees had laid green healing hands on his eyes, banishing the pictures of war. He had sucked strength from the green breasts of the hills.

Yet as strength flowed back to him and mind and spirit healed, McKay had grown steadily aware that the place was troubled; that its tranquillity was not perfect; that there was ferment of fear within it.

It was as though the trees had waited until he himself had become whole before they made their own unrest known to him. Now they were trying to tell him something; there was a shrillness as of apprehension, of anger, in the whispering of the leaves, the needled chanting of the pines.

And it was this that had kept McKay at the inn—a definite consciousness of appeal, consciousness of something wrong—something wrong that he was being asked to right. He strained his ears to catch words in the rustling branches, words that trembled on the brink of his human understanding.

Never did they cross that brink.

Gradually he had orientated himself, had focused himself, so he believed, to the point of the valley's unease.

On all the shores of the lake there were but two dwellings. One was the inn, and around the inn the trees clustered protectively, confiding; friendly. It was as though they had not only accepted it, but had made it part of themselves.

Not so was it of the other habitation. Once it had been the hunting lodge of long dead lords; now it was half ruined, forlorn. It stood across the lake almost exactly opposite the inn and back upon the slope a half mile from the shore. Once there had been fat fields around it and a fair orchard.

The forest had marched down upon them. Here and there in the fields, scattered pines and poplars stood like soldiers guarding some outpost; scouting parties of saplings lurked among the gaunt and broken fruit trees. But the forest had not had its way unchecked; ragged stumps showed where those who dwelt in the old lodge had cut down the invaders, blackened patches of the woodland showed where they had fired the woods.

Here was the conflict he had sensed. Here the green folk of the forest were both menaced and menacing; at war. The lodge was a fortress beleaguered by the woods, a fortress whose garrison sallied forth with axe and torch to take their toll of the besiegers.

Yet McKay sensed the inexorable pressing-in of the forest; he saw it as a green army ever filling the gaps in its enclosing ranks, shooting its seeds into the cleared places, sending its roots out to sap them; and armed always with a crushing patience, a patience drawn from the stone breasts of the eternal hills.

He had the impression of constant regard of watchfulness, as though night and day the forest kept its myriads of eyes upon the lodge; inexorably, not to be swerved from its purpose. He had spoken of this impression to the inn keeper and his wife, and they had looked at him oddly.

"Old Polleau does not love the trees, no," the old man had said. "No, nor do his two sons. They do not love the trees—and very certainly the trees do not love them."

Between the lodge and the shore, marching down to the verge of the lake was a singularly beautiful little coppice of silver birches and firs. The coppice stretched for perhaps a quarter of a mile, was not more than a hundred feet or two in depth, and it was not alone the beauty of its trees but their curious grouping that aroused McKay's interest so vividly. At each end of the coppice were a dozen or more of the glistening needled firs, not clustered but spread out as though in open marching order; at widely spaced intervals along its other two sides paced single firs. The birches, slender and delicate, grew within the guard of these sturdier trees, yet not so thickly as to crowd each other.

To McKay the silver birches were for all the world like some gay caravan of lovely demoiselles under the protection of debonair knights. With that odd other sense of his he saw the birches as delectable damsels, merry and laughing — the pines as lovers, troubadours in their green-needled mail. And when the winds blew and the crests of the trees bent under them, it was as though dainty demoiselles picked up fluttering, leafy skirts, bent leafy hoods and danced while the knights of the firs drew closer round them, locked arms with theirs and danced with them to the roaring horns of the winds. At such times he almost heard sweet laughter from the birches, shoutings from the firs.

Of all the trees in that place McKay loved best this little wood; had rowed across and rested in its shade, had dreamed there and, dreaming, had heard again elfin echoes of the sweet laughter; eyes closed, had heard mysterious whisperings and the sound of dancing feet light as falling leaves; had taken dream draught of that gaiety which was the soul of the little wood.

And two days ago he had seen Polleau and his two sons. McKay had been dreaming in the coppice all that afternoon. As dusk began to fall he had reluctantly arisen and begun the row back to the inn. When he had been a few hundred feet from shore three men had come out from the trees and had stood watching him—three grim, powerful men taller than the average French peasant.

He had called a friendly greeting to them, but they had not answered it; stood there, scowling. Then as he bent again to his oars, one of the sons had raised a hatchet and had driven it savagely into the trunk of a slim birch beside him. He thought he heard a thin wailing cry from the stricken tree, a sigh from all the little wood.

McKay had felt as though the keen edge had bitten into his own flesh.

"Stop that!" he had cried. "Stop it, damn you!"

For answer the son had struck again—and never had McKay seen hate etched so deep as on his face as he struck. Cursing, a killing rage in heart, had swung the boat around, raced back to shore. He had heard the hatchet strike again and again and, close now to shore, had heard a crackling and over it once more the thin, high wailing. He had turned to look.

The birch was tottering, was falling. But as it had fallen he had seen a curious thing. Close beside it grew one of the firs, and, as the smaller tree crashed over, it dropped upon the fir like a fainting maid in the arms of a lover. And as it lay and trembled there, one of the great branches of the fir slipped from under it, whipped out and smote the hatchet wielder a crushing blow upon the head, sending him to earth.

It had been, of course, only the chance blow of a bough, bent by pressure of the fallen tree and then released as that tree slipped down. But there had been such suggestion of conscious action in the branch's recoil, so much of bitter anger in it, so much, in truth, had it been like the vengeful blow of a man that McKay had felt an eerie prickling of his scalp, his heart had missed its beat.

For a moment Polleau and the standing son had stared at the sturdy fir with the silvery birch lying on its green breast and folded in, shielded by, its needled boughs as though—again the swift impression came to McKay—as though it were a wounded maid stretched on breast, in arms, of knightly lover. For a long moment father and son had stared.

Then, still wordless but with that same bitter hatred on both their faces, they had stopped and picked up the other and with his arms around the neck of each had borne him limply away.

McKay, sitting on the balcony of the inn that morning, went over and over that scene; realized more and more clearly the human aspect of fallen birch and clasping fir, and the conscious deliberateness of the fir's blow. And during the two days that had elapsed since then, he had felt the unease of the trees increase, their whispering appeal became more urgent.

What were they trying to tell him? What did they want him to do?

Troubled, he stared across the lake, trying to pierce the mists that hung over it and hid the opposite shore. And suddenly it seemed that he heard the coppice calling him, felt it pull the point of his attention toward it irresistibly, as the lodestone swings and holds the compass needle.

The coppice called him, bade him come to it.

Instantly McKay obeyed the command; he arose and walked down to the boat landing; he stepped into his skin and began to row across the lake. As his oars touched the water his trouble fell from him. In its place flowed peace and a curious exaltation.

The mist was thick upon the lake. There was no breath of wind, yet the mist billowed and drifted, shook and curtained under the touch of unfelt airy hands.

They were alive—the mists; they formed themselves into fantastic palaces past whose opalescent facades he saw; they built themselves into hills and valleys and circled plains whose floors were rippling silk. Tiny rainbows gleamed out among them, and upon the water prismatic patches shone and spread like spilled wine of opals. He had the illusion of vast distances—the hills of mist were real mountains, the valleys between them were not illusory. He was a colossus cleaving through some elfin world. A trout broke, and it was like leviathan leaping from the fathomless deep. Around the arc of its body rainbows interlaced and then dissolved into rain of softly gleaming gems—diamonds in dance with sapphires, flame-hearted rubies and pearls with shimmering souls of rose. The fish vanished, diving cleanly without sound; the jewelled bows vanished with it; a tiny irised whirlpool swirled for an instant where trout and flashing arcs had been.

Nowhere was there sound. He let his oars drop and leaned forward, drifting. In the silence, before him and around him, he felt opening the gateways of an unknown world.

And suddenly he heard the sound of voices, many voices; faint at first and murmurous; louder they became, swiftly; women's voices sweet and lilting and mingled with them the deeper tones of men. Voices that lifted and fell in a wild, gay chanting through whose joyesse ran undertones both of sorrow and of rage — as though færy weavers threaded through silk spun of sunbeams sombre strands dipped in the black of graves and crimson strands stained in the red of wrathful sunsets.

He drifted on, scarce daring to breathe lest even that faint sound break the elfin song. Closer it rang and clearer; and now he became aware that the speed of his boat was increasing, that it was no longer drifting; that it was as though the little waves on each side were pushing him ahead with soft and noiseless palms. His boat grounded and as it rustled along over the smooth pebbles of the beach the song ceased.

McKay half arose and peered before him. The mists were thicker here but he could see the outlines of the coppice. It was like looking at it through many curtains of fine gauze; its trees seemed shifting, ethereal, unreal. And moving among the trees were figures that threaded the boles and flitted in rhythmic measures like the shadows of leafy boughs swaying to some cadenced wind.

93

He stepped ashore and made his way slowly toward them. The mists dropped behind him, shutting off all sight of shore.

The rhythmic flittings ceased; there was now no movement as there was no sound among the trees—yet he felt the little woods abrim with watching life. McKay tried to speak; there was a spell of silence on his mouth.

"You called me. I have come to listen to you—to help you if I can."

The words formed within his mind, but utter them he could not. Over and over he tried, desperately; the words seemed to die before his lips could give them life.

A pillar of mist whirled forward and halted, eddying half an arm length away. And suddenly out of it peered a woman's face, eyes level with his own. A woman's face— yes; but McKay, staring into those strange eyes probing his, knew that face though it seemed it was that of no woman of human breed. They were without pupils, the irises deer-like and of the soft green of deep forest dells; within them sparkled tiny star points of light like motes in a moon beam. The eyes were wide and set far apart beneath a broad, low brow over which was piled braid upon braid of hair of palest gold, braids that seemed spun of shining ashes of gold. Her nose was small and straight, her mouth scarlet and exquisite. The face was oval, tapering to a delicately pointed chin.

Beautiful was that face, but its beauty was an alien one; elfin. For long moments the strange eyes thrust their gaze deep into his. Then out of the mist two slender white arms stole, the hands long, fingers tapering. The tapering fingers touched his ears.

"He shall hear," whispered the red lips.

Immediately from all about him a cry arose; in it was the whispering and rustling of the leaves beneath the breath of the winds, the shrilling of the harp strings of the boughs, the laughter of hidden brooks, the shoutings of waters flinging themselves down to deep and rocky pools—the voices of the woods made articulate.

"He shall hear!" they cried.

The long white fingers rested on his lips, and their touch was cool as bark of birch on cheek after some long upward climb through forest; cool and subtly sweet.

"He shall speak," whispered the scarlet lips.

"He shall speak!" answered the wood voices again, as though in litany.

"He shall see," whispered the woman and the cool fingers touched his eyes.

"He shall see!" echoed the wood voices.

The mists that had hidden the coppice from McKay wavered, thinned and were gone. In their place was a limpid, translucent, palely green ether, faintly luminous— as though he stood within some clear wan emerald. His feet pressed a golden moss spangled with tiny starry bluets. Fully revealed before him was the woman of the strange eyes and the face of elfin beauty. He dwelt for a moment upon the slender shoulders, the firm small tip-tilted breasts, the willow litheness of her body. From neck to knees a smock covered her, sheer and silken and delicate as though spun of cobwebs; through it her body gleamed as though fire of the young Spring moon ran in her veins.

Beyond her, upon the golden moss were other women like her, many of them; they stared at him with the same wide set green eyes in which danced the clouds of sparkling moonbeam motes; like her they were crowned with glistening, pallidly golden hair; like hers too were their oval faces with the pointed chins and perilous elfin beauty. Only where she stared at him gravely, measuring him, weighing him — there were those of these her sisters whose eyes were mocking; and those whose eyes called to him with a weirdly tingling allure, their mouths athirst; those whose eyes looked upon him with curiosity alone and those whose great eyes pleaded with him, prayed to him.

Within that pellucid, greenly luminous air McKay was abruptly aware that the trees of the coppice still had a place. Only now they were spectral indeed; they were like white shadows cast athwart a glaucous screen; trunk and bough, twig and leaf they arose around him and they were as though etched in air by phantom craftsmen — thin, unsubstantial; they were ghost trees rooted in another space.

Suddenly he was aware that there were men among the women; men whose eyes were set wide apart as were theirs, as strange and pupilless as were theirs but with irises of brown and blue; men with pointed chins and oval faces, broad shouldered and clad in kirtles of darkest green; swarthy-skinned men muscular and strong, with that same little grace of the women—and like them of a beauty alien and elfin.

McKay heard a little wailing cry. He turned. Close beside him lay a girl clasped in the arms of one of the swarthy, green-clad men. She lay upon his breast. His eyes were filled with a black flame of wrath, and hers were misted, anguished. For an instant McKay had a glimpse of the birch old Polleau's son had sent crashing down into the boughs of the fir. He saw birch and fir as immaterial outlines around the man and girl. For an instant girl and man and birch and fir seemed one and the same. The scarlet-lipped woman touched his shoulder, and the confusion cleared.

"She withers," sighed the woman, and in her voice McKay heard a faint rustling as of mournful leaves. "Now is it not pitiful that she withers—our sister who was so young, so slender and so lovely?"

McKay looked again at the girl. The white skin seemed shrunken; the moon radiance that gleamed through the bodies of the others in hers was dim and pallid; her slim arms hung listlessly; her body drooped. The mouth too was wan and parched, the long and misted green eyes dull. The palely golden hair lustreless, and dry. He looked on slow death—a withering death.

"May the arm that struck her down wither!" the green-clad man who held her shouted, and in his voice McKay heard a savage strumming as of winter winds through bleak boughs: "May his heart wither and the sun blast him! May the rain and the waters deny him and the winds scourge him!"

"I thirst," whispered the girl.

There was a stirring among the watching women. One came forward holding a chalice that was like thin leaves turned to green crystal. She paused beside the trunk of one of the spectral trees, reached up and drew down to her a branch. A slim girl with half-frightened, half-resentful eyes glided to her side and threw her arms around the ghostly bole. The woman with the chalice bent the branch and cut it deep with what seemed an arrow-shaped flake of jade. From the wound a faintly opalescent liquid slowly filled the cup. When it was filled the woman beside McKay stepped forward and pressed her own long hands around the bleeding branch. She stepped away and McKay saw that the stream had ceased to flow. She touched the trembling girl and unclasped her arms.

"It is healed," said the woman gently. "And it was your turn, little sister. The wound is healed. Soon, you will have forgotten."

The woman with the chalice knelt and set it to the wan, dry lips of her who was — withering. She drank of it, thirstily, to the last drop. The misty eyes cleared, they sparkled; the lips that had been so parched and pale grew red, the white body gleamed as though the waning light had been fed with new.

"Sing, sisters," she cried, and shrilly. "Dance for me, sisters!"

Again burst out that chant McKay had heard as he had floated through the mists upon the lake. Now, as then, despite his opened ears, he could distinguish no words, but clearly he understood its mingled themes—the joy of Spring's awakening, rebirth, with the green life streaming singing up through every bough, swelling the buds, burgeoning with tender leaves the branches; the dance of the trees in the scented winds of Spring; the drums of the jubilant rain on leafy hoods; passion of Summer sun pouring its golden flood down upon the trees; the moon passing with stately step and slow and green hands stretching up to her and drawing from her breast milk of silver fire; riot of wild gay winds with their mad pipings and strummings;—soft interlacing of boughs, the kiss of amorous leaves—all these and more, much more that McKay could not understand since it dealt with hidden, secret things for which man has no images, were in that chanting.

And all these and more were in the measures, the rhythms of the dancing of those strange, green eyed women and brown skinned men; something incredibly ancient yet young as the speeding moment, something of a world before and beyond man.

McKay listened, McKay watched, lost in wonder; his own world more than half forgotten; his mind meshed in web of green sorcery.

The woman beside him touched his arm. She pointed to the girl.

"Yet she withers," she said. "And not all our life, if we poured it through her lips, could save her."

He looked; he saw that the red was draining slowly from the girl's lips, the luminous life tides waning; the eyes that had been so bright were misting and growing dull once more, suddenly a great pity and a great rage shook him. He knelt beside her, took her hands in his.

"Take them away! Take away your hands! They burn me!" she moaned.

"He tries to help you," whispered the green-clad man, gently. But he reached over and drew McKay's hands away.

"Not so can you help her," said the woman.

"What can I do?" McKay arose, looked helplessly from one to the other. "What can I do to help?"

The chanting died, the dance stopped. A silence fell and he felt upon him the eyes of all. They were tense— waiting. The woman took his hands. Their touch was cool and sent a strange sweetness sweeping through his veins.

"There are three men yonder," she said. "They hate us. Soon we shall be as she is there—withering. They have sworn it, and as they have sworn so will they do. Unless—"

She paused; and McKay felt the stirrings of a curious unease. The moonbeam dancing motes in her eyes had changed to tiny sparklings of red. In a way, deep down, they terrified him—those red sparklings.

"Three men?"—in his clouded mind was the memory of Polleau and his two strong sons. "Three men," he repeated, stupidly—"But what are three men to you who are so many? What could three men do against those stalwart gallants of yours?"

"No," she shook her head. "No—there is nothing our—men—can do; nothing that we can do. Once, night and day, we were gay. Now we fear—night and day. They mean to destroy us. Our kin have warned us. And our kin cannot help us. Those three are masters of blade and flame. Against blade and flame we are helpless."

"Blade and flame!" echoed the listeners. "Against blade and flame we are helpless."

"Surely will they destroy us," murmured the woman. "We shall wither all of us. Like her there, or burn— unless—"

Suddenly she threw white arms around McKay's neck. She pressed her lithe body close to him. Her scarlet mouth sought and found his lips and clung to them. Through all

McKay's body ran swift, sweet flames, green fire of desire. His own arms went round her, crushed her to him.

"You shall not die!" he cried. "No—by God, you shall not!"

She drew back her head, looked deep into his eyes.

"They have sworn to destroy us," she said, "and soon. With blade and flame they will destroy us—these three— unless—"

"Unless?" he asked, fiercely.

"Unless you—slay them first!" she answered.

A cold shock ran through McKay, chilling the green sweet fires of his desire. He dropped his arm from around the woman; thrust her from him. For an instant she trembled before him.

"Slay!" he heard her whisper—and she was gone. The spectral trees wavered; their outlines thickened out of immateriality into substance. The green translucence darkened. He had a swift vertiginous moment as though he swung between two worlds. He closed his eyes. The vertigo passed and he opened them, looked around him.

McKay stood on the lakeward skirts of the little coppice. There were no shadows flitting, no sign of the white women and the swarthy, green-clad men. His feet were on green moss; gone was the soft golden carpet with its blue starlets. Birches and firs clustered solidly before him. At his left was a sturdy fir in whose needled arms a broken birch tree lay withering. It was the birch that Polleau's men had so wantonly slashed down. For an instant he saw within the fir and birch the immaterial outlines of the green-clad man and the slim girl who withered. For that instant birch and fir and girl and man seemed one and the same. He stepped back, and his hands touched the smooth, cool bark of another birch that rose close at his right.

Upon his hands the touch of that bark was like — was like? — yes, curiously was it like the touch of the long slim hands of the woman of the scarlet lips. But it gave him none of that alien rapture, that pulse of green life her touch had brought. Yet, now as then, the touch steadied him. The outlines of girl and man were gone.

He looked upon nothing but a sturdy fir with a withering birch fallen into its branches.

McKay stood there, staring, wondering, like a man who has but half awakened from dream. And suddenly a little wind stirred the leaves of the rounded birch beside him. The leaves murmured, sighed. The wind grew stronger and the leaves whispered.

"Slay!" he heard them whisper — and again: "Slay! Help us! Slay!"

And the whisper was the voice of the woman of the scarlet lips!

Rage, swift and unreasoning, sprang up in McKay. He began to run up through the coppice, up to where he knew was the old lodge in which dwelt Polleau and his sons. And as he ran the wind blew stronger, and louder and louder grew the whisperings of the trees.

"Slay!" they whispered. "Slay them! Save us! Slay!"

"I will slay! I will save you!" McKay, panting, hammer pulse beating in his ears, rushing through the woods heard himself answering that ever louder, ever more insistent command. And in his mind was but one desire—to clutch the throats of Polleau and his sons, to crack their necks; to stand by them then and watch them wither; wither like that slim girl in the arms of the green-clad man.

So crying, he came to the edge of the coppice and burst from it out into a flood of sunshine. For a hundred feet he ran, and then he was aware that the whispering command was stilled; that he heard no more that maddening rustling of wrathful leaves. A spell seemed to have been loosed from him; it was as though he had broken through some web of sorcery. McKay stopped, dropped upon the ground, buried his face in the grasses.

He lay there, marshalling his thoughts into some order of sanity. What had he been about to do? To rush berserk upon those three who lived in the old lodge and—kill them! And for what? Because that elfin, scarlet-lipped woman whose kisses he still could feel upon his mouth had bade him! Because the whispering trees of the little wood had maddened him with that same command!

And for this he had been about to kill three men!

What were that woman and her sisters and the green-clad swarthy gallants of theirs? Illusions of some waking dream—phantoms born of the hypnosis of the swirling mists through which he had rowed and floated across the lake? Such things were not uncommon. McKay knew of those who by watching the shifting clouds could create and dwell for a time with wide open eyes within some similar land of fantasy; knew others who needed but to stare at smoothly falling water to set themselves within a world of waking dream; there were those who could summon dreams by gazing into a ball of crystal, others found their phantoms in saucers of shining ebon ink.

Might not the moving mists have laid those same hypnotic fingers upon his own mind—and his love for the trees the sense of appeal that he had felt so long and his memory of the wanton slaughter of the slim birch have all combined to paint upon his drugged consciousness the phantasms he had beheld?

Then in the flood of sunshine the spell had melted, his consciousness leaped awake?

McKay arose to his feet, shakily enough. He looked back at the coppice. There was no wind now, the leaves were silent, motionless. Again he saw it as the caravan of demoiselles with their marching knights and troubadours. But no longer was it gay. The words of the scarlet-lipped woman came back to him—that gaiety had fled and fear had taken its place. Dream phantom or—dryad, whatever she was, half of that at least was truth.

He turned, a plan forming in his mind. Reason with himself as he might, something deep within him stubbornly asserted the reality of his experience. At any rate, he told himself, the little wood was far too beautiful to be despoiled. He would put aside the experience as dream — but he would save the little wood for the essence of beauty that it held in its green cup.

The old lodge was about a quarter of a mile away. A path led up to it through the ragged fields. McKay walked up the path, climbed rickety steps and paused, listening. He heard voices and knocked. The door was flung open and old Polleau stood there, peering at him through half shut, suspicious eyes. One of the sons stood close behind him. They stared at McKay with grim, hostile faces.

He thought he heard a faint, far off despairing whisper from the distant wood. And it was as though the pair in the doorway heard it too, for their gaze shifted from him to the coppice, and he saw hatred flicker swiftly across their grim faces; their gaze swept back to him.

"What do you want?" demanded Polleau, curtly.

"I am a neighbor of yours, stopping at the inn —" began McKay, courteously.

"I know who you are," Polleau interrupted brusquely. "But what is it that you want?"

"I find the air of this place good for me," McKay stifled a rising anger. "I am thinking of staying for a year or more until my health is fully recovered. I would like to buy some of your land and build me a lodge upon it."

"Yes, M'sieu?" there was acid politeness now in the powerful old man's voice. "But is it permitted to ask why you do not remain at the inn? Its fare is excellent and you are well liked there."

"I have desire to be alone," replied McKay. "I do not like people too close to me. I would have my own land, and sleep under my own roof."

"But why come to me?" asked Polleau. "There are many places upon the far side of the lake that you could secure. It is happy there, and this side is not happy, M'sieu. But tell me, what part of my land is it that you desire?"

"That little wood yonder," answered McKay, and pointed to the coppice.

"Ah! I thought so!" whispered Polleau, and between him and his sons passed a look of bitter understanding. He looked at McKay, sombrely.

"That wood is not for sale, M'sieu," he said at last. "I can afford to pay well for what I want," said McKay. "Name your price."

"It is not for sale," repeated Polleau, stolidly, "at any price."

"Oh, come," laughed McKay, although his heart sank at the finality in that answer. "You have many acres and what is it but a few trees? I can afford to gratify my fancies. I will give you all the worth of your other land for it."

"You have asked what that place that you so desire is, and you have answered that it is but a few trees," said Polleau, slowly, and the tall son behind him laughed, abruptly, maliciously. "But it is more than that, M'sieu—Oh, much more than that. And you know it, else why would you pay such price? Yes, you know it—since you know also that we are ready to destroy it, and you would save it. And who told you all that, M'sieu?" he snarled.

There was such malignance in the face thrust suddenly close to McKay's, teeth bared by uplifted lip, that involuntarily he recoiled.

"But a few trees!" snarled old Polleau. "Then who told him what we mean to do—eh, Pierre?"

Again the son laughed. And at that laughter McKay felt within him resurgence of his own blind hatred as he had fled through the whispering wood. He mastered himself, turned away, there was nothing he could do—now. Polleau halted him.

"M'sieu," he said. "Wait. Enter. There is something I would tell you; something too I would show you. Something, perhaps, that I would ask you."

He stood aside, bowing with a rough courtesy. McKay walked through the doorway. Polleau with his son followed him. He entered a large, dim room whose ceiling was spanned with smoke blackened beams. From these beams hung onion strings and herbs and smoke cured meats. On one side was a wide fireplace. Huddled beside it sat Polleau's other son. He glanced up as they entered and McKay saw that a bandage covered one side of his head, hiding his left eye. McKay recognized him as the one who had cut down the slim birch. The blow of the fir, he reflected with a certain satisfaction, had been no futile one.

Old Polleau strode over to that son.

"Look, M'sieu," he said and lifted the bandage.

McKay with a faint tremor of horror, saw a gaping blackened socket, red rimmed and eyeless.

"Good God, Polleau!" he cried. "But this man needs medical attention. I know something of wounds. Let me go across the lake and bring back my kit. I will attend him."

Old Polleau shook his head, although his grim face for the first time softened. He drew the bandages back in place.

"It heals," he said. "We have some skill in such things. You saw what did it. You watched from your boat as the cursed tree struck him. The eye was crushed and lay upon his cheek. I cut it away. Now he heals. We do not need your aid, M'sieu."

"Yet he ought not have cut the birch," muttered McKay, more to himself than to be heard.

"Why not?" asked old Polleau, fiercely. "Since it hated him."

109

McKay stared at him. What did this old peasant know? The words strengthened that deep stubborn conviction that what he had seen and heard in the coppice had been actuality — no dream. And still more did Polleau's next words strengthen that conviction.

"M'sieu," he said, "you come here as ambassador — of a sort. The wood has spoken to you. Well, as ambassador I shall speak to you. Four centuries my people have lived in this place. A century we have owned this land. M'sieu, in all those years there has been no moment that the trees have not hated us — nor we the trees.

"For all those hundred years there have been hatred and battle between us and the forest. My father, M'sieu, was crushed by a tree; my elder brother crippled by another. My father's father, woodsman that he was, was lost in the forest — he came back to us with mind gone, raving of wood women who had bewitched and mocked him, luring him into swamp and fen and tangled thicket, tormenting him. In every generation the trees have taken their toll of us — women as well as men — maiming or killing us."

"Accidents," interrupted McKay. "This is childish, Polleau. You cannot blame the trees."

"In your heart you do not believe so," said Polleau. "Listen, the feud is an ancient one. Centuries ago it began when we were serfs, slaves of the nobles. To cook, to keep us warm in winter, they let us pick up the fagots, the dead branches and twigs that dropped from the trees. But if we cut down a tree to keep us warm, to keep our women and

our children warm, yes, if we but tore down a branch —
they hanged us, or they threw us into dungeons to rot, or
whipped us till our backs were red lattices.

"They had their broad fields, the nobles — but we must
raise our food in the patches where the trees disdained to
grow. And if they did thrust themselves into our poor
patches, then, M'sieu, we must let them have their way —
or be flogged, or be thrown into the dungeons or be
hanged.

"They pressed us in — the trees," the old man's voice
grew sharp with fanatic hatred. "They stole our fields and
they took the food from the mouths of our children; they
dropped their fagots to us like dole to beggars; they
tempted us to warmth when the cold struck our bones —
and they bore us as fruit a-swing at the end of the
foresters' ropes if we yielded to their tempting.

"Yes, M'sieu — we died of cold that they might live!
Our children died of hunger that their young might find
root space! They despised us — the trees! We died that they
might live — and we were men!

"Then, M'sieu came the Revolution and the freedom.
Ah, M'sieu, then we took our toll! Great logs roaring in the
winter cold — no more huddling over the alms of fagots.
Fields where the trees had been — no more starving of our
children that theirs might live. Now the trees were the
slaves and we the masters.

"And the trees knew and they hated us!

"But blow for blow, a hundred of their lives for each life of ours—we have returned their hatred. With axe and torch we have fought them—

"The trees!" shrieked Polleau, suddenly, eyes blazing red rage, face writhing, foam at the corners of his mouth and gray hair clutched in rigid hands—"The cursed trees! Armies of the trees creeping—creeping—closer, ever closer—crushing us in! Stealing our fields as they did of old! Building their dungeon round us as they built of old the dungeons of stone! Creeping—creeping! Armies of trees! Legions of trees! The trees! The cursed trees!"

McKay listened, appalled. Here was crimson heart of hate. Madness! But what was at the root of it? Some deep inherited instinct, coming down from forefathers who had hated the forest as the symbol of their masters. Forefathers whose tides of hatred had overflowed to the green life on which the nobles had laid their tabu—as one neglected child will hate the favorite on whom love and gifts are lavished? In such warped minds the crushing fall of a tree, the maiming sweep of a branch, might well appear as deliberate, the natural growth of the forest seem the implacable advance of an enemy.

And yet—the blow of the fir as the cut birch fell had been deliberate! and there had been those women of the wood—

"Patience," the standing son touched the old man's shoulder. "Patience! Soon we strike our blow."

Some of the frenzy died out of Polleau's face.

"Though we cut down a hundred," he whispered, "By the hundred they return! But one of us, when they strike — he does not return. No! They have numbers and they have — time. We are now but three, and we have little time. They watch us as we go through the forest, alert to trip, to strike, to crush!

"But M'sieu," he turned blood-shot eyes to McKay. "We strike our blow, even as Pierre has said. We strike at the coppice that you so desire. We strike there because it is the very heart of the forest. There the secret life of the forest runs at full tide. We know — and you know! Something that, destroyed, will take the heart out of the forest — will make it know us for its masters."

"The women!" the standing son's eyes glittered, "I have seen the women there! The fair women with the shining skins who invite — and mock and vanish before hands can seize them."

"The fair women who peer into our windows in the night — and mock us!" muttered the eyeless son.

"They shall mock no more!" shouted Polleau, the frenzy again taking him. "Soon they shall lie, dying! All of them — all of them! They die!"

He caught McKay by the shoulders, shook him like a child.

"Go tell them that!" he shouted. "Say to them that this very day we destroy them. Say to them it is we who will laugh when winter comes and we watch their round white bodies blaze in this hearth of ours and warm us! Go—tell them that!"

He spun McKay around, pushed him to the door, opened it and flung him staggering down the steps. He heard the tall son laugh, the door close. Blind with rage he rushed up the steps and hurled himself against the door. Again the tall son laughed. McKay beat at the door with clenched fists, cursing. The three within paid no heed. Despair began to dull his rage. Could the trees help him— counsel him? He turned and walked slowly down the field path to the little wood.

Slowly and ever more slowly he went as he neared it. He had failed. He was a messenger bearing a warrant of death. The birches were motionless; their leaves hung listlessly. It was as though they knew he had failed. He paused at the edge of the coppice. He looked at his watch, noted with faint surprise that already it was high noon. Short shrift enough had the little wood. The work of destruction would not be long delayed.

McKay squared his shoulders and passed in between the trees. It was strangely silent in the coppice. And it was mournful. He had a sense of life brooding around him, withdrawn into itself; sorrowing. He passed through the silent, mournful wood until he reached the spot where the rounded, gleaming barked tree stood close to the fir that held the withering birch. Still there was no sound, no movement. He laid his hands upon the cool bark of the rounded tree.

"Let me see again!" he whispered. "Let me hear! Speak to me!"

There was no answer. Again and again he called. The coppice was silent. He wandered through it, whispering, calling. The slim birches stood, passive with limbs and leaves adroop like listless arms and hands of captive maids awaiting with dull woe the will of conquerors. The firs seemed to crouch like hopeless men with heads in hands. His heart ached to the woe that filled the little wood, this hopeless submission of the trees.

When, he wondered, would Polleau strike. He looked at his watch again; an hour had gone by. How long would Polleau wait? He dropped to the moss, back against a smooth bole.

And suddenly it seemed to McKay that he was a madman—as mad as Polleau and his sons. Calmly, he went over the old peasant's indictment of the forest; recalled the face and eyes filled with the fanatic hate. Madness! After all, the trees were—only trees. Polleau and his sons—so he reasoned—had transferred to them the bitter hatred their forefathers had felt for those old lords who had enslaved them; had laid upon them too all the bitterness of their own struggle to exist in this high forest land. When they struck at the trees, it was the ghosts of these forefathers striking at the nobles who had oppressed them; it was themselves striking against their own destiny. The trees were but symbols. It was the warped minds of Polleau and his sons that clothed them in false semblance of conscious life in blind striving to wreak vengeance against the ancient masters and the destiny that had made their lives hard and unceasing battle against Nature. The nobles were long dead; destiny can be brought to grips by no man. But the trees were here and alive. Clothed in mirage, through them the driving lust for vengeance could be sated.

And he, McKay, was it not his own deep love and sympathy for the trees that similarly had clothed them in that false semblance of conscious life? Had he not built his own mirage? The trees did not really mourn, could not suffer, could not—know. It was his own sorrow that he had transferred to them; only his own sorrow that he felt echoing back to him from them.

The trees were—only trees.

Instantly, upon the heels of that thought, as though it were an answer, he was aware that the trunk against which he leaned was trembling; that the whole coppice was trembling; that all the little leaves were shaking, tremulously.

McKay, bewildered, leaped to his feet. Reason told him that it was the wind—yet there was no wind!

And as he stood there, a sighing arose as though a mournful breeze were blowing through the trees—and again there was no wind!

Louder grew the sighing and within it now faint wailings.

"They come! They come! Farewell, sisters! Sisters—farewell!"

Clearly he heard the mournful whispers.

McKay began to run through the trees to the trail that led out to the fields of the old lodge. And as he ran the wood darkened as though clear shadows gathered in it, as though vast unseen wings hovered over it. The trembling of the coppice increased; bough touched bough, clung to each other; and louder became the sorrowful crying:

"Farewell, sister! Sister — farewell!"

McKay burst out into the open. Halfway between him and the lodge were Polleau and his sons. They saw him; they pointed and lifted mockingly to him bright axes. He crouched, waiting for them to come, all fine spun theories gone and rising within him that same rage that hours before had sent him out to slay.

So crouching, he heard from the forested hills a roaring clamor. From every quarter it came, wrathful, menacing; like the voices of legions of great trees bellowing through the horns of tempest. The clamor maddened McKay; fanned the flame of rage to white heat.

If the three men heard it, they gave no sign. They came on steadily, jeering at him, waving their keen blades. He ran to meet them.

"Go back!" he shouted. "Go back, Polleau! I warn you!"

"He warns us!" jeered Polleau. "He — Pierre, Jean — he warns us!"

The old peasant's arm shot out and his hand caught McKay's shoulder with a grip that pinched to the bone. The arm flexed and hurled him against the unmaimed son. The son caught him, twisted him about and whirled him headlong a dozen yards, crashing him through the brush at the skirt of the wood.

McKay sprang to his feet howling like a wolf. The clamor of the forest had grown stronger.

"Kill!" it roared. "Kill!"

The unmaimed son had raised his axe. He brought it down upon the trunk of a birch, half splitting it with one blow. McKay heard a wail go up from the little wood. Before the axe could be withdrawn he had crashed a fist in the axe wielder's face. The head of Polleau's son rocked back; he yelped, and before McKay could strike again had wrapped strong arms around him, crushing breath from him. McKay relaxed, went limp, and the son loosened his grip. Instantly McKay slipped out of it and struck again, springing aside to avoid the rib breaking clasp. Polleau's son was quicker than he, the long arms caught him. But as the arms tightened, there was the sound of sharp splintering and the birch into which the axe had bitten toppled. It struck the ground directly behind the wrestling men. Its branches seemed to reach out and clutch at the feet of Polleau's son.

He tripped and fell backward, McKay upon him. The shock of the fall broke his grip and again McKay writhed free. Again he was upon his feet, and again Polleau's strong son, quick as he, faced him. Twice McKay's blows found their mark beneath his heart before once more the long arms trapped him. But their grip was weaker; McKay felt that now his strength was equal.

Round and round they rocked, McKay straining to break away. They fell, and over they rolled and over, arms and legs locked, each striving to free a hand to grip the other's throat. Around them ran Polleau and the one-eyed son, shouting encouragement to Pierre, yet neither daring to strike at McKay lest the blow miss and be taken by the other.

And all that time McKay heard the little wood shouting. Gone from it now was all mournfulness, all passive resignation. The wood was alive and raging. He saw the trees shake and bend as though torn by a tempest. Dimly he realized that the others must hear none of this, see none of it; as dimly wondered why this should be.

"Kill!" shouted the coppice—and over its tumult he heard the roar of the great forest:

"Kill! Kill!"

He became aware of two shadowy shapes, shadowy shapes of swarthy green-clad men, that pressed close to him as he rolled and fought.

"Kill!" they whispered. "Let his blood flow! Kill! Let his blood flow!"

He tore a wrist free from the son's clutch. Instantly he felt within his hand the hilt of a knife.

"Kill!" whispered the shadowy men.

"Kill!" shrieked the coppice.

"Kill!" roared the forest.

McKay's free arm swept up and plunged the knife into the throat of Polleau's son! He heard a choking sob; heard Polleau shriek; felt the hot blood spurt in face and over hand; smelt its salt and faintly acrid odor. The encircling arms dropped from him; he reeled to his feet.

As though the blood had been a bridge, the shadowy men leaped from immateriality into substances. One threw himself upon the man McKay had stabbed; the other hurled upon old Polleau. The maimed son turned and fled, howling with terror. A white woman sprang out from the shadow, threw herself at his feet, clutched them and brought him down. Another woman and another dropped upon him. The note of his shrieking changed from fear to agony; then died abruptly into silence.

And now McKay could see none of the three, neither old Polleau or his sons, for the green-clad men and the white women covered them!

McKay stood stupidly, staring at his red hands. The roar of the forest had changed to a deep triumphal chanting. The coppice was mad with joy. The trees had become thin phantoms etched in emerald translucent air as they had been when first the green sorcery had enmeshed him. And all around him wove and danced the slim, gleaming women of the wood.

They ringed him, their song bird-sweet and shrill; jubilant. Beyond them he saw gliding toward him the woman of the misty pillars whose kisses had poured the sweet green fire into his veins. Her arms were outstretched to him, her strange wide eyes were rapt on his, her white body gleamed with the moon radiance, her red lips were parted and smiling—a scarlet chalice filled with the promise of undreamed ecstasies. The dancing circle, chanting, broke to let her through.

Abruptly, a horror filled McKay. Not of this fair woman, not of her jubilant sisters — but of himself.

He had killed! And the wound the war had left in his soul, the wound he thought had healed, had opened.

He rushed through the broken circle, thrust the shining woman aside with his blood-stained hands and ran, weeping, toward the lake shore. The singing ceased. He heard little cries, tender, appealing; little cries of pity; soft voices calling on him to stop, to return. Behind him was the sound of little racing feet, light as the fall of leaves upon the moss.

McKay ran on. The coppice lightened, the beach was before him. He heard the fair woman call him, felt the touch of her hand upon his shoulder. He did not heed her. He ran across the narrow strip of beach, thrust his boat out into the water and wading through the shallows threw himself into it.

He lay there for a moment, sobbing; then drew himself up, caught at the oars. He looked back at the shore now a score of feet away. At the edge of the coppice stood the woman, staring at him with pitying, wise eyes. Behind her clustered the white faces of her sisters, the swarthy faces of the green-clad men.

"Come back!" the woman whispered, and held out to him slender arms.

McKay hesitated, his horror lessening in that clear, wise, pitying gaze. He half swung the boat around. His gaze dropped upon his blood-stained hands and again the hysteria gripped him. One thought only was in his mind— to get far away from where Polleau's son lay with his throat ripped open, to put the lake between that body and him.

Head bent low, McKay bowed to the oars, skimming swiftly outward. When he looked up a curtain of mist had fallen between him and the shore. It hid the coppice and from beyond it there came to him no sound. He glanced behind him, back toward the inn. The mists swung there, too, concealing it.

McKay gave silent thanks for these vaporous curtains that hid him from both the dead and the alive. He slipped limply under the thwarts. After a while he leaned over the side of the boat and, shuddering, washed the blood from his hands. He scrubbed the oar blades where his hands had left red patches. He ripped the lining out of his coat and drenching it in the lake he cleansed his face. He took off the stained coat, wrapped it with the lining round the anchor stone in the skiff and sunk it in the lake. There were other stains upon his shirt; but these he would have to let be.

For a time he rowed aimlessly, finding in the exertion a lessening of his soul sickness. His numbed mind began to function, analyzing his plight, planning how to meet the future—how to save him.

What ought he do? Confess that he had killed Polleau's son? What reason could he give? Only that he had killed because the man had been about to cut down some trees—trees that were his father's to do with as he willed!

And if he told of the wood woman, the wood women, the shadowy shapes of their green gallants who had helped him—who would believe?

They would think him mad—mad as he half believed himself to be.

No, none would believe him. None! Nor would confession bring back life to him he had slain. No; he would not confess.

But stay—another thought came! Might he not be—accused? What actually had happened to old Polleau and his other son? He had taken it for granted that they were dead; that they had died under those bodies white and swarthy. But had they? While the green sorcery had meshed him he had held no doubt of this—else why the jubilance of the little wood, the triumphant chanting of the forest?

Were they dead—Polleau and the one-eyed son? Clearly it came to him that they had not heard as he had, had not seen as he had. To them McKay and his enemy had been but two men battling, in a woodland glade; nothing more than that—until the last! Until the last? Had they seen more than that even then?

No, all that he could depend upon as real was that he had ripped out the throat of one of old Polleau's sons. That was the one unassailable verity. He had washed the blood of that man from his hands and his face.

All else might have been mirage—but one thing was true. He had murdered Polleau's son!

Remorse? He had thought that he had felt it. He knew now that he did not; that he had no shadow of remorse for what he had done. It had been panic that had shaken him, panic realization of the strangenesses, reaction from the battle lust, echoes of the war. He had been justified in that—execution. What right had those men to destroy the little wood; to wipe wantonly its beauty away?

None! He was glad that he had killed!

At that moment McKay would gladly have turned his boat and raced away to drink of the crimson chalice of the wood woman's lips. But the mists were raising, He saw that he was close to the landing of the inn.

There was no one about. Now was his time to remove the last of those accusing stains. After that—

Quickly he drew up, fastened the skiff, slipped unseen to his room. He locked the door, started to undress. Then sudden sleep swept over him like a wave, drew him helplessly down into ocean depths of sleep.

A knocking at the door awakened McKay, and the innkeeper's voice summoned him to dinner. Sleepily, he answered, and as the old man's footsteps died away, he roused himself. His eyes fell upon his shirt and the great stains now rusty brown. Puzzled, he stared at them for a moment, then full memory clicked back in place.

He walked to the window. It was dusk. A wind was blowing and the trees were singing, all the little leaves dancing; the forest hummed a cheerful vespers. Gone was all the unease, all the inarticulate trouble and the fear. The forest was tranquil and it was happy.

He sought the coppice through the gathering twilight. Its demoiselles were dancing lightly in the wind, leafy hoods dipping, leafy skirts ablow. Beside them marched the green troubadours, carefree, waving their needled arms. Gay was the little wood, gay as when its beauty had first drawn him to it.

McKay undressed, hid the stained shirt in his travelling trunk, bathed and put on a fresh outfit, sauntered down to dinner. He ate excellently. Wonder now and then crossed his mind that he felt no regret, no sorrow even, for the man he had killed. Half he was inclined to believe it all a dream — so little of any emotion did he feel. He had even ceased to think of what discovery might mean.

His mind was quiet; he heard the forest chanting to him that there was nothing he need fear; and when he sat for a time that night upon the balcony a peace that was half an ecstasy stole in upon him from the murmuring woods and enfolded him. Cradled by it he slept dreamlessly.

McKay did not go far from the inn that next day. The little wood danced gaily and beckoned him, but he paid no heed. Something whispered to wait, to keep the lake between him and it until word came of what lay or had lain there. And the peace still was on him.

Only the old innkeeper seemed to grow uneasy as the hours went by. He went often to the landing, scanning the further shore.

"It is strange," he said at last to McKay as the sun was dipping behind the summits. "Polleau was to see me here today. He never breaks his word. If he could not come he would have sent one of his sons."

McKay nodded, carelessly.

"There is another thing I do not understand," went on the old man. "I have seen no smoke from the lodge all day. It is as though they were not there."

"Where could they be?" asked McKay, indifferently.

"I do not know," the voice was more perturbed. "It all troubles me, M'sieu. Polleau is hard, yes; but he is my neighbor. Perhaps an accident—"

"They would let you know soon enough if there was anything wrong," McKay said.

"Perhaps, but—" the old man hesitated. "If he does not come tomorrow and again I see no smoke I will go to him," he ended.

McKay felt a little shock run through him—tomorrow then he would know, definitely know, what it was that had happened in the little wood.

"I would if I were you," he said. "I'd not wait too long either. After all—well, accidents do happen."

"Will you go with me, M'sieu," asked the old man.

"No!" whispered the warning voice within McKay. "No! Do not go!"

"Sorry," he said, aloud. "But I've some writing to do. If you should need me send back your man. I'll come."

And all that night he slept, again dreamlessly, while the crooning forest cradled him.

The morning passed without sign from the opposite shore. An hour after noon he watched the old innkeeper and his man row across the lake. And suddenly McKay's composure was shaken, his serene certainty wavered. He unstrapped his field glasses and kept them on the pair until they had beached the boat and entered the coppice. His heart was beating uncomfortably, his hands felt hot and his lips dry. He scanned the shore. How long had they been in the wood? It must have been an hour! What were they doing there? What had they found? He looked at his watch, incredulously. Less than fifteen minutes had passed.

Slowly the seconds ticked by. And it was all of an hour indeed before he saw them come out upon the shore and drag their boat into the water. McKay, throat curiously dry, a deafening pulse within his ears, steadied himself; forced himself to stroll leisurely down to the landing.

"Everything all right?" he called as they were near. They did not answer; but as the skiff warped against the landing they looked up at him and on their faces were stamped horror and a great wonder.

"They are dead, M'sieu," whispered the innkeeper. "Polleau and his two sons—all dead!"

McKay's heart gave a great leap, a swift faintness took him.

"Dead!" he cried. "What killed them?"

"What but the trees, M'sieu?" answered the old man, and McKay thought his gaze dwelt upon him strangely. "The trees killed them. See—we went up the little path through the wood, and close to its end we found it blocked by fallen trees. The flies buzzed round those trees, M'sieu, so we searched there. They were under them, Polleau and his sons. A fir had fallen upon Polleau and had crushed in his chest. Another son we found beneath a fir and upturned birches. They had broken his back, and an eye had been torn out—but that was no new wound, the latter." He paused.

128

"It must have been a sudden wind," said his man. "Yet I never knew of a wind like that must have been. There were no trees down except those that lay upon them. And of those it was as though they had leaped out of the ground! Yes, as though they had leaped out of the ground upon them. Or it was as though giants had torn them out for clubs. They were not broken—their roots were bare—"

"But the other son—Polleau had two?"—try as he might, McKay could not keep the tremor out of his voice.

"Pierre," said the old man, and again McKay felt that strange quality in his gaze. "He lay beneath a fir. His throat was torn out!"

"His throat torn out!" whispered McKay, His knife! The knife that had been slipped into his hand by the shadowy shapes!

"His throat was torn out," repeated the innkeeper. "And in it still was the broken branch that had done it. A broken branch, M'sieu, pointed as a knife. It must have caught Pierre as the fir fell and ripping through his throat—been broken off as the tree crashed."

McKay stood, mind whirling in wild conjecture. "You said—a broken branch?" McKay asked through lips gone white.

"A broken branch, M'sieu," the innkeeper's eyes searched him. "It was very plain—what it was that happened. Jacques," he turned to his man. "Go up to the house."

He watched until the man shuffled out of sight. "Yet not all plain, M'sieu," he spoke low to McKay. "For in Pierre's hand I found — this."

He reached into a pocket and drew out a button from which hung a strip of cloth. Cloth and button had once been part of that blood-stained coat which McKay had sunk within the lake; torn away no doubt when death had struck Polleau's son!

McKay strove to speak. The old man raised his hand. Button and cloth fell from it, into the water. A wave took it and floated it away; another and another. They watched it silently until it had vanished.

"Tell me nothing, M'sieu," the old innkeeper turned to him, "Polleau was hard and hard men, too, were his sons. The trees hated them. The trees killed them. And now the trees are happy. That is all. And the — souvenir — is gone. I have forgotten I saw it. Only M'sieu would better also — go."

That night McKay packed. When dawn had broken he stood at his window, looked long at the little wood. It was awakening, stirring sleepily like drowsy delicate demoiselles. He drank in its beauty — for the last time; waved it farewell.

McKay breakfasted well. He dropped into the driver's seat; set the engine humming. The old innkeeper and his wife, solicitous as ever for his welfare, bade him Godspeed. On both their faces was full friendliness — and in the old man's eyes somewhat of puzzled awe.

His road lay through the thick forest. Soon inn and lake were far behind him.

And singing went McKay, soft whisperings of leaves following him, glad chanting of needled pines; the voice of the forest tender, friendly, caressing — the forest pouring into him as farewell gift its peace, its happiness, its strength.

THE LAST POET AND THE ROBOTS

NARODNY, THE RUSSIAN, sat in his laboratory. Narodny's laboratory was a full mile under earth. It was one of a hundred caverns, some small and some vast, cut out of the living rock. It was a realm of which he was sole ruler. In certain caverns garlands of small suns shone; and in others little moons waxed and waned over earth; and there was a cavern in which reigned perpetual dawn, dewy, over lily beds and violets and roses; and another in which crimson sunsets baptized in the blood of slain day dimmed and died and were born again behind the sparkling curtains of the aurora. And there was one cavern ten miles from side to side in which grew flowering trees and trees which bore fruits unknown to man for many generations. Over this great orchard one yellow sun-like orb shone, and clouds trailed veils of rain upon the trees and miniature thunder drummed at Narodny's summoning.

Narodny was a poet—the last poet. He did not write his poems in words but in colors, sounds, and visions made material. Also he was a great scientist. In his Peculiar field the greatest. Thirty years before, Russia's Science Council had debated whether to grant him the leave of absence he had asked, or to destroy him. They knew him to be unorthodox. How deadly so they did not know, else after much deliberation they would not have released him. It must be remembered that of all nations, Russia then was the most mechanized; most robot-ridden.

Narodny did not hate mechanization. He was indifferent to it. Being truly intelligent he hated nothing, Also he was indifferent to the whole civilization man had developed and into which he had been born. He had no feeling of kinship to humanity. Outwardly, in body, he belonged to the species. Not so in mind. Like Loeb, a thousand years before, he considered mankind a race of crazy half-monkeys, intent upon suicide. Now and then, out of the sea of lunatic mediocrity, a wave uplifted that held for a moment a light from the sun of truth—but soon it sank back and the light was gone. Quenched in the sea of stupidity. He knew that he was one of those waves.

He had gone, and he had been lost to sight by all. In a few years he was forgotten. Fifteen years ago, unknown and under another name, he had entered America and secured rights to a thousand acres in what of old had been called Westchester. He had picked this place because investigation had revealed to him that of ten localities on this planet it was most free from danger of earthquake or similar seismic disturbance. The man who owned it had been whimsical; possibly an atavist—like Narodny, although Narodny would never have thought of himself as that. At any rate, instead of an angled house of glass such as the thirtieth century built, this man had reconstructed a rambling old stone house of the nineteenth century. Few people lived upon the open land in those days; most had withdrawn into the city-states. New York, swollen by its meals of years, was a fat belly full of mankind still many miles away. The land around the house was forest covered.

A week after Narodny had taken this house, the trees in front of it had melted away leaving a three-acre, smooth field. It was not as though they had been cut, but as though they had been dissolved. Later that night a great airship had appeared upon this field—abruptly, as though it had blinked out of another dimension. It was rocket-shaped but noiseless. And immediately a fog had fallen upon airship and house, hiding them. Within this fog, if one could have seen, was a wide tunnel leading from the air-cylinder's door to the door of the house. And out of the airship came swathed figures, ten of them, who walked along that tunnel, were met by Narodny, and the door of the old house closed on them.

A little later they returned, Narodny with them, and out of an opened hatch of the airship rolled a small flat car on which was a mechanism of crystal cones rising around each other to a central cone some four feet high. The cones were upon a thick base of some glassy material in which was imprisoned a restless green radiance. Its rays did not penetrate that which held it, but it seemed constantly seeking, with suggestion of prodigious force, to escape. For hours the strange thick fog held. Twenty miles up in the far reaches of the stratosphere, a faintly sparkling cloud grew, like a condensation of cosmic dust. And just before dawn the rock of the hill behind the house melted away like a curtain that had covered a great tunnel. Five of the men came out of the house and went into the airship. It lifted silently from the ground, slipped into the aperture and vanished. There was a whispering sound, and when it had died away the breast of the hill was whole again. The rocks had been drawn together like a closing curtain and boulders studded it as before. That the breast was now slightly concave where before it had been convex, none would have noticed.

For two weeks the sparkling cloud was observed far up in the stratosphere, was commented upon idly, and then was seen no more. Narodny's caverns were finished.

Half of the rock from which they had been hollowed had gone with that sparkling cloud. The balance, reduced to its primal form of energy, was stored in blocks of the vitreous material that had supported the cones, and within them it moved as restlessly and always with that same suggestion of prodigious force. And it was force, unthinkably potent; from it came the energy that made the little suns and moons, and actuated the curious mechanisms that regulated pressure in the caverns, supplied the air, created the rain, and made of Narodny's realm a mile deep under earth the Paradise of poetry, of music, of color and of form which he had conceived in his brain and with the aid of those ten others had caused to be.

Now of the ten there is no need to speak further. Narodny was the Master. But three, like him, were Russians; two were Chinese; of the remaining five, three were women—one German in ancestry, one Basque, one an Eurasian; a Hindu who traced his descent from the line of Gautama; a Jew who traced his from Solomon.

All were one with Narodny in indifference to the world; each with him in his viewpoint on life; and each and all lived in his or her own Eden among the hundred caverns except when it interested them to work with each other. Time meant nothing to them. Their researches and discoveries were solely for their own uses and enjoyments. If they had given them to the outer world they would have only been ammunition for warfare either between men upon Earth or men against some other planet. Why hasten humanity's suicide? Not that they would have felt regret at the eclipse of humanity. But why trouble to expedite it? Time meant nothing to them because they could live as long as they desired — barring accident. And while there was rock in the world, Narodny could convert it into energy to maintain his Paradise — or to create others.

The old house began to crack and crumble. It fell — much more quickly than the elements could have brought about its destruction. Then trees grew among the ruins of its foundations; and the field that had been so strangely cleared was overgrown with trees. The land became a wood in a few short years; silent except for the roar of an occasional rocket passing over it and the songs of birds that had found there a sanctuary.

But deep down in earth, within the caverns, were music and song and mirth and beauty. Gossamer nymphs circled under the little moons. Pan piped. There was revelry of antique harvesters under the small suns. Grapes grew and ripened, were pressed, and red and purple wine was drunk by Bacchantes who fell at last asleep in the arms of fauns and satyrs. Oreads danced under the pale moon-bows and sometimes Centaurs wheeled and trod archaic measures beneath them to the drums of their hoofs upon the mossy floor. The old Earth lived again.

Narodny listened to drunken Alexander raving to Thais among the splendors of conquered Persepolis; and he heard the crackling of the flames that at the whim of the courtesan destroyed it. He watched the siege of Troy and counted with Homer the Achæan ships drawn up on the strand before Troy's walls; or saw with Herodotus the tribes that marched behind Xerxes—the Caspians in their cloaks of skin with their bows of cane; the Ethiopians in the skins of leopards with spears of antelope horns; the Libyans in their dress of leather with javelins made hard by fire; the Thracians with the heads of foxes upon their heads; the Moschians who wore helmets made of wood and the Cabalians who wore the skulls of men. For him the Eleusinian and the Osirian mysteries were re-enacted, and he watched the women of Thrace tear to fragments Orpheus, the first great musician. At his will, he could see the rise and fall of the Empire of the Aztecs, the Empire of the Incas; or beloved Cæsar slain in Rome's Senate; or the archers at Agincourt; or the Americans in Belleau Wood. Whatever man had written—whether poets, historians, philosophers or scientists—his strangely shaped mechanisms could bring before him, changing the words into phantoms real as though living.

He was the last and greatest of the poets—but also he was the last and greatest of the musicians. He could bring back the songs of ancient Egypt, or the chants of more ancient Ur. The songs that came from Moussorgsky's soul of Mother-earth, the harmonies of Beethoven's deaf ear, or the chants and rhapsodies from the heart of Chopin. He could do more than restore the music of the past. He was master of sound. To him, the music of the spheres was real. He could take the rays of the stars and planets and weave them into symphonies. Or convert the sun's rays into golden tones no earthly orchestras had ever expressed. And the silver music of the moon—the sweet music of the moon of spring, the full-throated music of the harvest moon, the brittle crystalling music of the winter moon with its arpeggios of meteors—he could weave into strains such as no human ears had ever heard.

So Narodny, the last and greatest of poets, the last and greatest of musicians, the last and greatest of artists—and in his inhuman way, the greatest of scientists—lived with the ten of his choosing in his caverns. And, with them, he consigned the surface of earth and all who dwelt upon it to a negative Hell—Unless something happening there might imperil his Paradise!

Aware of the possibility of that danger, among his mechanisms were those which brought to eyes and ears news of what was happening on earth's surface. Now and then, they amused themselves with these.

It so happened that on that night when the Warper of Space had dealt his blow at the space ships and had flung a part of the great Crater of Copernicus into another dimension, Narodny had been weaving the rays of Moon, Jupiter and Saturn into Beethoven's Moonlight Sonata. The moon was a four-day crescent. Jupiter was at one cusp, and Saturn hung like a pendant below the bow. Shortly Orion would stride across the Heavens and bright Regulus and red Aldebaran, the Eye of the Bull, would furnish him with other chords of starlight remoulded into sound.

Suddenly the woven rhythms were ripped — hideously. A devastating indescribable dissonance invaded the cavern. Beneath it, the nymphs who had been dancing languorously to the strains quivered like mist wraiths in a sudden blast and were gone: the little moons flared, then ceased to glow. The tonal instruments were dead. And Narodny was felled as though by a blow.

After a time the little moons began to glow again, but dimly; and from the tonal mechanisms came broken, crippled music. Narodny stirred and sat up, his lean, high-cheeked face more Satanic than ever. Every nerve was numb; then as they revived, agony crept along them. He sat, fighting the agony, until he could summon help. He was answered by one of the Chinese, and soon Narodny was himself again.

He said: "It was a spatial disturbance, Lao. And it was like nothing I have ever known. It came in upon the rays, of that I am sure. Let us look out upon the moon."

They passed to another cavern and stood before an immense television screen. They adjusted it, and upon it appeared the moon, rapidly growing larger as though it were hurtling toward them. Then upon the screen appeared a space ship speeding earthward. They focused upon it, and opened it to their vision; searching it until they came to the control room where were Bartholomew, James Tarvish and Martin, their gaze upon Earth rapidly and more rapidly expanding in the heavens. Narodny and the Chinese watched them, reading their lips. Tarvish said: "Where can we land, Martin? The robots will be watching for us everywhere. They will see to it that we are destroyed before we can give our message and our warning to the world. They control the governments—or at least control them sufficiently to seize us upon landing. And if we should escape and gather men around us, then it means civil war and that in turn means fatal delay in the building of the space fleet—even if we should win."

Martin said: "We must land safely—escape the robots—find some to control or destroy them. God, Tarvish—you saw what that devil they call the Wrongness of Space can do. He threw the side of the crater out of our dimension as a boy would throw a stone into a pond!"

Bartholomew said: "He could take Earth and break it up piecemeal—"

Narodny and Lao looked at each other. Narodny said: "That is enough. We know." The Chinese nodded. Narodny said: "I estimated that they would reach Earth in four hours." Again Lao nodded. Narodny said: "We will talk to them, Lao; although I had thought we were done with mankind. I do not like this which they call so quaintly the Wrongness of Space—nor the stone he threw into my music."

They brought a smaller screen into position before the larger one. They oriented it to the speeding space

Ship and stepped in front of it. The small screen shimmered with whirling vortices of pallid blue luminescence; the vortices drew together and became one vast cone that reached on and on to the greater screen as though not feet but thousands of miles separated them. And as the tip of the cone touched the control room of the space ship mirrored in the screen, Tarvish, upon the actual ship, gripped Martin's arm.

"Look there!"

There was an eddying in the air, like that over roads on a hot summer day. The eddying became a shimmering curtain of pallid blue luminescence—steadied until it was an oval doorway opening into vast distances. And then abruptly, within that doorway, stood two men—one tall and lean and saturnine with the sensitive face of a dreamer and the other a Chinese, his head a great yellow dome and on his face the calm of Buddha—and it was strange indeed to see in the cavern of earth these same two men standing before the blue-coned screen and upon the greater one their images within the imaged room on which the tip of the cone rested.

Narodny spoke, and in his voice there was a human indifference and sureness that chilled them, yet gave them courage. He said: "We mean you no harm. You cannot harm us. We have long been withdrawn from men. What happens on the surface of Earth means nothing to us. What may happen beneath the surface means much. Whatever it is you have named the Wrongness of Space has already annoyed me. I perceive that he can do more than annoy. I gather that the robots in one way or another are on his side. You are against him. Therefore, our first step must be to help you against the robots. Place me in possession of all facts. Be brief, for we cannot maintain our position here for more than half an hour without discomfort."

Martin said: "Whoever you are, wherever you are, we trust you. Here is the story—"

For fifteen minutes Narodny and the Chinese listened to their tale of struggle against the robots, of their escape and of the blasting of Copernicus in the effort of the Wrongness of Space to prevent their return.

Narodny said: "Enough. Now I understand. How long can you remain in space? I mean—what are your margins of power and of food?"

Martin answered: "Six days."

Narodny said: "Ample time for success—or failure. Remain aloft for that time, then descend to where you started—"

Suddenly he smiled: "I care nothing for mankind—yet I would not harm them, willingly. And it has occurred to me that I owe them, after all, a great debt. Except for them—I would not be. Also, it occurs to me that the robots have never produced a poet, a musician, an artist—" He laughed: "But it is in my mind that they are capable of one great art at least! We shall see."

The oval was abruptly empty; then it too was gone. Bartholomew said: "Call the others. I am for obeying. But they must know." And when the others had heard, they too voted to obey, and the space ship, course changed, began to circle, as slowly as it could, the earth.

Down in the chamber of the screens, Narodny laughed and laughed again. He said: "Lao, is it that we have advanced so in these few years? Or that men have retrogressed? No, it is this curse of mechanization that destroys imagination. For look you, how easy is this problem of the robots. They began as man-made machines. Mathematical, soulless, insensible to any emotion. So was primal matter of which all on earth are made, rock and water, tree and grass, metal, animal, fish, worm, and men. But somewhere, somehow, something was added to this primal matter, combined with it — used it. It was what we call life. And life is consciousness. And therefore largely emotion. Life established its rhythm — and its rhythm being different in rock and crystal, metal, fish, and so on, and man, we have these varying things.

"Well, it seems that life has begun to establish its rhythm in the robots. Consciousness has touched them. The proof? They have established the idea of common identity — group consciousness. That in itself involves emotion. But they have gone further. They have attained the instinct of self-preservation. And that, my wise friend, connotes fear — fear of extinction. And fear connotes anger, hatred, arrogance — and many other things. The robots, in short, have become emotional to a degree. And therefore vulnerable to whatever may amplify and control their emotions. They are no longer mechanisms.

"So, Lao, I have in mind an experiment that will provide me study and amusement through many years.

Originally, the robots are the children of mathematics. I ask — to what is mathematics most closely related. I answer — to rhythm — to sound — to sounds which will raise to the nth degree the rhythms to which they will respond. Both mathematically and emotionally,"

Lao said: "The sonic sequences?"

Narodny answered: "Exactly. But we must have a few with which to experiment. To do that means to dissolve the upper gate. But that is nothing. Tell Maringy and Euphroysne to do it. Net a ship and bring it here. Bring it down gently. You will have to kill the men in it, of course, but do it mercifully. Then let them bring me the robots. Use the green flame on one or two — the rest will follow, I'll warrant you."

The hill behind where the old house had stood trembled. A circle of pale green light gleamed on its breast. It dimmed, where it had been was the black mouth of a tunnel. An airship, half-rocket, half-winged, making its way to New York, abruptly dropped, circled, and streaked back. It fell gently like a moth, close to the yawning mouth of the tunnel.

Its door opened, and out came two men, pilots, cursing. There was a little sigh from the tunnel's mouth and a silvery misty cloud sped from it, over the pilots and straight through the opened door. The pilots staggered and crumpled to the ground. In the airship half a dozen other men slumped to the floor, smiled, and died.

There were a full score robots in the ship. They stood, looking at the dead men and at each other. Out of the tunnel came two figures swathed in metallic glimmering robes. They entered the ship. One said:

"Robots, assemble."

The metal men stood, motionless. Then one sent out a shrill call. From all parts of the ship the metal men moved. They gathered behind the one who had sent the call. They stood behind him, waiting.

In the hand of one of those who had come from the tunnel was what might have been an antique flash-light. From it sped a thin green flame. It struck the foremost robot on the head, sliced down from the head to base of trunk. Another flash, and the green flame cut him from side to side. He fell, sliced by that flame into four parts. The four parts lay, inert as their metal, upon the floor of the compartment.

One of the shrouded figures said: "Do you want further demonstration—or will you follow us?"

The robots put heads together; whispered. Then one said: "We will follow." '

They marched into the tunnel, the robots making no resistance nor effort to escape. Again there was the sighing, and the rocks closed the tunnel mouth. They game to a place whose floor sank with them until it had reached the caverns. The machine-men still went docilely. Was it because of curiosity mixed with disdain for these men whose bodies could be broken so easily by one blow of the metal appendages that served them for arms? Perhaps.

They came to the cavern where Narodny and the others awaited them. Marinoff led them in and halted them. These were the robots used in the flying ships — their heads cylindrical, four arm appendages, legs triple jointed, torsos slender. The robots, it should be understood, were differentiated in shape according to their occupations. Narodny said:

"Welcome, robots. Who is your leader?"

One answered: "We have no leaders. We act as one."

Narodny laughed: "Yet by speaking for them you have shown yourself leader. Step closer. Do not fear — yet."

The robot said: "We feel no fear. Why should we? Even if you should destroy us who are here, you cannot destroy the billions of us outside. Nor can you breed fast enough, become men soon enough, to cope with us who enter into life strong and complete from the beginning."

He flecked an appendage toward Narodny and there was contempt in the gesture. But before he could draw it back a bracelet of green flame circled it at the shoulder. It had darted like a thrown loop from something in Narodny's hand. The robot's arm dropped clanging to the floor, cleanly severed. The robot stared at it unbelievingly, threw forward his other three arms to pick it up. Again the green flame encircled them, encircled also his legs above the second joints. The robot crumpled and pitched forward, crying in high-pitched shrill tones to the others.

Swiftly the green flame played among them. Legless, armless, some decapitated, all the robots fell except two.

"Two will be enough," said Narodny. "But they will not need arms — only feet."

The flashing green bracelets encircled the appendages and excised them. The pair were marched away. The bodies of the others were taken apart, studied and under Narodny's direction curious experiments were made. Music filled the cavern, strange chords, unfamiliar progressions, shattering arpeggios and immense vibrations of sound that could be felt but not heard by the human ear. And finally this last deep vibration burst into hearing as a vast drone, hummed up and up into swift tingling tempest of crystalline brittle notes, and still ascending passed into shrill high pipings, and continued again unheard, as had the prelude to the droning. And thence it rushed back, the piping and the crystalline storm reversed, into the drone and the silence — then back and up.

And the bodies of the broken robots began to quiver, to tremble, as though every atom within them were in ever increasing, rhythmic motion. Up rushed the music and down — again and again. If ended abruptly in midflight with one crashing note.

The broken bodies ceased their quivering. Tiny star-shaped cracks appeared in their metal. Once more the note sounded and the cracks widened. The metal splintered.

Narodny said: "Well, there is the frequency for the rhythm of our robots. The destructive unison. I hope for the sake of the world outside it is not also the rhythm of many of their buildings and bridges. But after all, in any war there must be casualties on both sides."

Lao said: "Earth will be an extraordinary spectacle for a few days."

Narodny said: "It's going to be an extraordinarily uncomfortable Earth for a few days, and without doubt many will die and many more go mad. But is there any other way?"

There was no answer. He said; "Bring in the two robots." They brought them in.

Narodny said: "Robots—were there ever any of you who could poetize?"

They answered: "What is poetize?" Narodny laughed: "Never mind. Have you ever sung—made music—painted? Have you ever—dreamed?"

One robot said with cold irony: "Dreamed? No—for we do not sleep. We leave all that to men. It is why we have conquered them."

Narodny said, almost gently: "Not yet, robot. Have you ever—danced? No? It is an art you are about to learn."

The unheard note began, droned up and through the tempest and away and back again. And up and down—and up and down, though not so loudly as before. And suddenly the feet of the robots began to move, to shuffle. Their leg-joints bent; their bodies swayed. The note seemed to move now here and now there about the chamber, they always following it, grotesquely. Like huge metal marionettes, they followed it. The music ended in the crashing note. And it was as though every vibrating atom of the robot bodies had met some resistible obstruction. Their bodies quivered and from their voice mechanisms came a shriek that was a hideous blend of machine and life. Once more the drone, and once more and once more and again the abrupt stop. There was a brittle crackling all over the conical heads, all over the bodies. The star-shaped splinterings appeared. Once again the drone—but the two robots stood, unresponding. For through the complicated mechanisms which under their carapaces animated them were similar splinterings.

The robots were dead!

Narodny said: "By tomorrow we can amplify the sonar to make it effective in a 3000-mile circle. We will use the upper cavern, of course. Equally of course, it means we must take the ship out again. In three days, Marinoff, you should be able to cover the other continents. See to it that the ship is completely proof against the vibrations. To work. We must act quickly—before the robots can discover how to neutralize them."

It was exactly at noon next day that over all North America a deep unexplainable droning was heard. It seemed to come not only from deep within earth, but from every side. It mounted rapidly through a tempest of tingling crystalline notes into a shrill piping and was gone…then back it rushed from piping to the drone…then up and out and down…again and again. And over all North America the hordes of robots stopped in whatever they were doing. Stopped…and then began to dance. They danced in the airships and scores of those ships crashed before the human crews could gain control. They danced by the thousands in the streets of the cities—in grotesque rigadoons, in bizarre sarabands, with shuffle and hop, and jig the robots danced while the people fled in panic and hundreds of them were crushed and died in those panics. In the great factories, and in the tunnels of the lower cities, and in the mines—everywhere the sound was heard—and it was heard everywhere—the robots danced…to the piping of Narodny, the last great poet…the last great musician.

And then came the crashing note—and over all the country the dance halted. And began again…and ceased…and began again…

Until at last the streets, the lower tunnels of the lower levels, the mines, the factories, the homes, were littered with metal bodies shot through and through with star-shaped splinterings.

In the cities the people cowered, not knowing what blow was to fall upon them…or milled about in fear maddened crowds, and many more died…

Then suddenly the dreadful droning, the shattering tempest, the intolerable high piping ended. And everywhere the people fell, sleeping among the dead robots, as though they never had been strung to the point of breaking, sapped of strength and abruptly relaxed.

As though it had vanished, America was deaf to cables, to all communication beyond the gigantic circle of sound.

But that midnight over all Europe the drone sounded and Europe's robots began their dance of death...and when it had ended a strange and silent rocket ship that had hovered high above the stratosphere sped almost with the speed of light and hovered over Asia—and next day Africa heard the drone while the natives answered it with their tom-toms—then South America heard it and last of all far-off Australia...and everywhere terror trapped the peoples and panic and madness took their toll...

Until of all that animate metal horde that had tethered Earth and humanity there were a few scant hundreds left—escaped from the death dance through some variant in their constitution. And, awakening from that swift sleep, all over Earth those who had feared and hated the robots and their slavery rose against those who had fostered the metal domination, and blasted the robot factories to dust.

Again the hill above the caverns opened, the strange torpedo ship blinked into sight like a ghost, as silently as a ghost floated into the hill and the rocks closed behind it.

Narodny and the others stood before the gigantic television screen, shifting upon it images of city after city, country after country, over all Earth's surface. Lao, the Chinese, said: "Many men died, but many are left. They may not understand—but to them it was worth it."

Narodny mused: "It drives home the lesson, what man does not pay for, he values little. Our friends aloft will have little opposition now I think."

He shook his head, doubtfully, "But I still do not like that Wrongness of Space. I do not want my music spoiled again by him, Lao. Shall we hurl the Moon out of the universe, Lao?"

Lao laughed: "And what then would you do for moon-music?"

Narodny said: "True. Well, let us see what men can do. There is always time—perhaps."

The difficulties which beset humanity did not interest the poet Narodny. While the world governments were reorganized—factories turned out space ships for Earth's fleet—men were trained in handling these ships—supplies were gathered—weapons were perfected—and when the message from Luna, outlining the course to be followed and setting the starting date, arrived, the space fleet of Earth was ready to leave.

Narodny watched the ships take off. He shook his head, doubtfully. But soon harmonies were swelling through the great cavern of the orchards and nymphs and fauns dancing under the fragrant blossoming trees—and the world again forgotten by Narodny.

THE CHALLENGE FROM BEYOND[1]

[C.L. Moore]

GEORGE CAMPBELL OPENED SLEEP-FOGGED EYES upon darkness and lay gazing out of the tent flap upon the pale August night for some minutes before he roused enough even to wonder what had wakened him. There was in the keen, clear air of these Canadian woods a soporific as potent as any drug. Campbell lay quiet for a moment, sinking slowly back into the delicious borderlands of sleep, conscious of an exquisite weariness, an unaccustomed sense of muscles well used, and relaxed now into perfect ease. These were vacation's most delightful moments, after all — rest, after toil, in the clear, sweet forest night.

Luxuriously, as his mind sank backward into oblivion, he assured himself once more that three long months of freedom lay before him — freedom from cities and monotony, freedom from pedagogy and the University and students with no rudiments of interest in the geology

---

[1] *EDITOR'S NOTE: This story was written collaboratively, by five different authors, each taking a section in turn.*

he earned his daily bread by dinning into their obdurate ears. Freedom from—

Abruptly the delightful somnolence crashed about him. Somewhere outside the sound of tin shrieking across tin slashed into his peace. George Campbell sat up jerkily and reached for his flashlight. Then he laughed and put it down again, straining his eyes through the midnight gloom outside where among the tumbling cans of his supplies a dark anonymous little night beast was prowling. He stretched out a long arm and groped about among the rocks at the tent door for a missile. His fingers closed on a large stone, and he drew back his hand to throw.

But he never threw it. It was such a queer thing he had come upon in the dark. Square, crystal smooth, obviously artificial, with dull rounded corners. The strangeness of its rock surfaces to his fingers was so remarkable that he reached again for his flashlight and turned its rays upon the thing he held.

All sleepiness left him as he saw what it was he had picked up in his idle groping. It was clear as rock crystal, this queer, smooth cube. Quartz, unquestionably, but not in its usual hexagonal crystallized form. Somehow—he could not guess the method—it had been wrought into a perfect cube, about four inches in measurement over each worn face. For it was incredibly worn. The hard, hard crystal was rounded now until its corners were almost gone and the thing was beginning to assume the outlines of a sphere. Ages and ages of wearing, years almost beyond counting, must have passed over this strange clear thing.

But the most curious thing of all was that shape he could make out dimly in the heart of the crystal. For imbedded in its center lay a little disc of a pale and nameless substance with characters incised deep upon its quartz-enclosed surface. Wedge-shaped characters, faintly reminiscent of cuneiform writing.

George Campbell wrinkled his brows and bent closer above the little enigma in his hands, puzzling helplessly. How could such a thing as this have imbedded in pure rock crystal? Remotely a memory floated through his mind of ancient legends that called quartz crystals ice which had frozen too hard to melt again. Ice—and wedge-shaped cuneiforms—yes, didn't that sort of writing originate among the Sumerians who came down from the north in history's remotest beginnings to settle in the primitive Mesopotamian valley? Then hard sense regained control and he laughed. Quartz, of course, was formed in the earliest of earth's geological periods, when there was nothing anywhere but beat and heaving rock. Ice had not come for tens of millions of years after this thing must have been formed.

And yet—that writing. Man-made, surely, although its characters were unfamiliar save in their faint hinting at cuneiform shapes. Or could there, In a Paleozoic world, have been things with a written language who might have graven these cryptic wedges upon the quartz-enveloped disc he held? Or—might a thing like this have fallen meteor-like out of space into the unformed rock of a still molten world? Could it—

Then he caught himself up sharply and felt his ears going hot at the luridness of his own imagination. The silence and the solitude and the queer thing in his hands were conspiring to play tricks with his common sense. He shrugged and laid the crystal down at the edge of his pallet, switching off the light. Perhaps morning and a clear head would bring him an answer to the questions that seemed so insoluble now.

But sleep did not come easily. For one thing, it seemed to him as he flashed off the light, that the little cube had shone for a moment as if with sustained light before it faded into the surrounding dark. Or perhaps he was wrong. Perhaps It had been only his dazzled eyes that seemed to see the light forsake it reluctantly, glowing In the enigmatic deeps of the thing with queer persistence.

He lay there unquietly for a long while, turning the unanswered questions over and over in his mind. There was something about this crystal cube out of the unmeasured past, perhaps from the dawn of all history, that constituted a challenge that would not let him sleep.

[A. Merritt]

HE LAY THERE, it seemed to him, for hours. It had been the lingering light, the luminescence that seemed so reluctant to die, which held his mind. It was as though something in the heart of the cube had awakened, stirred drowsily, become suddenly alert…and Intent upon him.

Sheer fantasy, this. He stirred impatiently and flashed his light upon his watch. Close to one o'clock; three hours more before the dawn. The beam fell and was focused upon the warm crystal cube. He held it there closely, for minutes. He snapped It out, then watched.

There was no doubt about it now. As his eyes accustomed themselves to the darkness, he saw that the strange crystal was glimmering with tiny fugitive lights deep within it like threads of sapphire lightnings. They were at Its center and they seemed to him to come from the pale disk with Its disturbing markings. And the disc itself was becoming larger...the markings shifting shapes...the cube was growing...was it illusion brought about by the tiny lightnings...

He heard a sound. It was the very ghost of a sound, like the ghosts of harp strings being plucked with ghostly fingers. He bent closer. It came from the cube...

There was squeaking in the underbrush, a flurry of bodies and an agonized wailing like a child in death throes and swiftly stilled. Some small tragedy of the wilderness, killer and prey. He stepped over to where it had been enacted, but could see nothing. He again snapped off the flash and looked toward his tent. Upon the ground was a pale blue glimmering. It was the cube. He stooped to pick it up; then obeying some obscure warning, drew back his hand.

And again, he saw, its glow was dying. The tiny sapphire lightnings flashing fitfully, withdrawing to the disc from which they had come. There was no sound from it.

He sat, watching the luminescence glow and fade, glow and fade, but steadily becoming dimmer. It came to him that two elements were necessary to produce the phenomenon. The electric ray itself, and his own fixed attention. His mind must travel along the ray, fix itself upon the cube's heart, if its beat were to wax, until…what?

He felt a chill of spirit, as though from contact with some alien thing. It was alien, he knew it; not of this earth. Not of earth's life. He conquered his shrinking, picked up the cube and took It into the tent. It was neither warm nor cold; except for its weight he would not have known he held it. He put it upon the table, keeping the torch turned from it; then stepped to the flap of the tent and closed it.

He went back to the table, drew up the camp chair, and turned the flash directly upon the cube, focusing it so far as he could upon its heart. He sent all his will, all his concentration, along it; focusing will and sight upon the disc as he had the light.

As though at command, the sapphire lightnings burned forth. They burst from the disc into the body of the crystal cube, then beat back, bathing the disc and the markings. Again these began to change, shifting, moving, advancing, and retreating in the blue gleaming. They were no longer cuneiform. They were things…objects.

He heard the murmuring music, the plucked harp strings. Louder grew the sound and louder, and now all the body of the cube vibrated to their rhythm. The crystal walls were melting, growing misty as though formed of the mist of diamonds. And the disc Itself was growing…the shapes shifting, dividing and multiplying as though some door had been opened and Into it companies of phantasms were pouring. While brighter, more bright grew the pulsing light.

He felt swift panic, tried to withdraw sight and will, dropped the flash. The cube had no need now of the ray…and he could not withdraw…could not withdraw? Why, he himself was being sucked into that disc which was now a globe within which unnameable shapes danced to a music that bathed the globe with steady radiance.

There was no tent. There was only a vast curtain of sparkling mist behind which shone the globe… He felt himself drawn through that mist, sucked through it as if by a mighty wind, straight for the globe.

[H. P. Lovecraft]

AS THE MIST-BLURRED LIGHT of the sapphire suns grew more and more intense, the outlines of the globe ahead wavered and dissolved to a churning chaos. Its pallor and its motion and its music all blended themselves with the engulfing mist- bleaching It to a pale steel-colour and setting it undulantly in motion. And the sapphire suns, too, melted Imperceptibly into the greying infinity of shapeless pulsation.

Meanwhile the sense of forward, outward motion grew intolerably, incredibly, cosmically swift. Every standard of speed known to earth seemed dwarfed, and Campbell knew that any such flight in physical reality would mean instant death to a human being. Even as it was—in this strange, hellish hypnosis or nightmare—the quasi-visual impression of meteor-like hurtling almost paralyzed his mind. Though there were no real points of reference in the grey, pulsing void, he felt that he was approaching and passing the speed of light Itself. Finally his consciousness did go under—and merciful blackness swallowed everything.

It was very suddenly, and amidst the most impenetrable darkness, that thoughts and Ideas again came to George Campbell. Of how many moments—or years—or eternities—had elapsed since his flight through the grey void, he could form no estimate. He knew only that he seemed to be at rest and without pain. Indeed, the absence of all physical sensation was the salient quality of his condition. It made even the blackness seem less solidly black—suggesting as it did that he was rather a disembodied intelligence in a state beyond physical senses, than a corporeal being with senses deprived of their accustomed objects of perception. He could think sharply and quickly—almost preternaturally so—yet could form no idea whatsoever of his situation.

Half by instinct, he realised that he was not in his own tent. True, he might have awaked there from a nightmare to a world equally black; yet he knew this was not so. There was no camp cot beneath him—he had no hands to feel the blankets and canvas surface and flashlight that ought to be around him—there was no sensation of cold in the air—no flap through which he could glimpse the pale night outside…something was wrong, dreadfully wrong.

He cast his mind backward and thought of the fluorescent cube which had hypnotised him—of that, and all which had followed. He had known that his mind was going, yet had been unable to draw back. At the last moment there had been a shocking, panic fear—a subconscious fear beyond even that caused by the sensation of dæmonic flight. It had come from some vague flash or remote recollection—just what, he could not at once tell. Some cell-group In the back of his head had seemed to find a cloudily familiar quality In the cube— and that familiarity was fraught with dim terror. Now he tried to remember what the familiarity and the terror were.

Little by little it came to him. Once—long ago, in connection with his geological life-work—he had read of something like that cube. It had to do with those debatable and disquieting clay fragments called the Eltdown Shards, dug up from pre-carboniferous strata in southern England thirty years before. Their shape and markings were so queer that a few scholars hinted at artificiality, and made wild conjectures about them and their origin. They came, clearly, from a time when no human beings could exist on the globe—but their contours and figurings were damnably puzzling. That was how they got their name.

It was not, however, In the writings of any sober scientist that Campbell had seen that reference to a crystal, disc-holding globe. The source was far less reputable, and infinitely more vivid. About 1912 a deeply learned Sussex

clergyman of occultist leanings—the Reverend Arthur
Brooke Winters-Hall—had professed to Identify the
markings on the Eltdown Shards with some of the so-
called "pre-human hieroglyphs" persistently cherished
and esoterically handed down in certain mystical circles,
and had published at his own expense what purported to
be a "translation" of the primal and baffling
"inscriptions"—a "translation" still quoted frequently and
seriously by occult writers. In this "translation'—a
surprisingly long brochure In view of the limited number
of "shards" existing—had occurred the narrative,
supposedly of pre-human authorship, containing the now
frightening reference.

As the story went, there dwelt on a world—and
eventually on countless other worlds—of outer space a
mighty order of worm-like beings whose attainments and
whose control of nature surpassed anything within the
range of terrestrial imagination. They had mastered the art
of interstellar travel early in their career, and had peopled
every habitable planet in their own galaxy - killing off the
races they found.

Beyond the limits of their own galaxy—which was not
ours—they could not navigate in person; but in their quest
for knowledge of all space and time they discovered a
means of spanning certain transgalactic gulfs with their
minds. They devised peculiar objects—strangely energized
cubes of a curious crystal containing hypnotic talismen
and enclosed in space-resisting spherical envelopes of an
unknown substance—which could be forcibly expelled
beyond the limits of their universe, and which would
respond to the attraction of cool solid matter only.

These, of which a few would necessarily land on various inhabited worlds in outside universes, formed the ether-bridges needed for mental communication. Atmospheric friction burned away the protecting envelope, leaving the cube exposed and subject to discovery by the intelligent minds of the world where it fell. By its very nature, the cube would attract and rivet attention. This, when coupled with the action of light, was sufficient to set its special properties working.

The mind that noticed the cube would be drawn into it by the power of the disc, and would be sent on a thread of obscure energy to the place whence the disc had come — the remote world of the worm-like space explorers across stupendous galactic abysses. Received in one of the machines to which each cube was attuned, the captured mind would remain suspended without body or senses until examined by one of the dominant race. Then it would, by an obscure process of interchange, be pumped of all its contents. The investigator's mind would now occupy the strange machine while the captive mind occupied the interrogator's worm-like body. Then, in another interchange, the interrogator's mind would leap across boundless space to the captive's vacant and unconscious body on the trans-galactic world — animating the alien tenement as best It might, and exploring the alien world in the guise of one of its denizens.

When done with exploration, the adventurer would use the cube and its disc in accomplishing his return — and sometimes the captured mind would be restored safely to its own remote world. Not always, however, was the dominant race so kind. Sometimes, when a potentially important race capable of space travel was found, the worm-like folk would employ the cube to capture and annihilate minds by the thousands, and would extirpate the race for diplomatic reasons—using the exploring minds as agents of destruction.

In other cases sections of the worm-folk would permanently occupy a trans-galactic planet - destroying the captured minds and wiping out the remaining inhabitants preparatory to settling down in unfamiliar bodies. Never, however, could the parent civilization be quite duplicated In such a case; since the new planet would not contain all the materials necessary for the worm-race's arts. The cubes, for example, could be made only on the home planet.

Only a few of the numberless cubes sent forth ever found a landing and response on an inhabited world - since there was no such thing as aiming them at goals beyond sight or knowledge. Only three, ran the story, had ever landed on peopled worlds in our own particular universe. One of these had struck a planet near the galactic rim two thousand billion years ago, while another had lodged three billion years ago on a world near the centre of the galaxy. The third—and the only one ever known to have invaded the solar system—had reached our own earth 150,000,000 years ago.

It was with this latter that Dr. Winters-Hall's "translation" chiefly dealt. When the cube struck the earth, he wrote, the ruling terrestrial species was a huge, cone-shaped race surpassing all others before or since In mentality and achievements. This race was so advanced that it had actually sent minds abroad in both space and time to explore the cosmos, hence recognised something of what had happened when the cube fell from the sky and certain Individuals had suffered mental change after gazing at it.

Realising that the changed Individuals represented invading minds, the race's leaders had them destroyed — even at the cost of leaving the displaced minds exiled in alien space. They had had experience with even stranger transitions. When, through a mental exploration of space and time, they formed a rough Idea of what the cube was, they carefully hid the thing from light and sight, and guarded it as a menace. They did not wish to destroy a thing so rich in later experimental possibilities. Now and then some rash, unscrupulous adventurer would furtively gain access to it and sample its perilous powers despite the consequences — but all such cases were discovered, and safely and drastically dealt with.

Of this evil meddling the only bad result was that the worm-like outside race learned from the new exiles what had happened to their explorers on earth, and conceived a violent hatred of the planet and all its life-forms. They would have depopulated it if they could, and indeed sent additional cubes into space in the wild hope of striking it by accident in unguarded places — but that accident never came to pass.

The cone-shaped terrestrial beings kept the one existing cube in a special shrine as a relique and basis for experiments, till after æons it was lost amidst the chaos of war and the destruction of the great polar city where it was guarded. When, fifty million years ago, the beings sent their minds ahead into the infinite future to avoid a nameless peril of inner earth, the whereabouts of the sinister cube from space were unknown.

This much, according to the learned occultist, the Eltdown Shards had said. What now made the account so obscurely frightful to Campbell was the minute accuracy with which the alien cube had been described. Every detail tallied — dimensions, consistency, heiroglyphed central disc, hypnotic effects. As he thought the matter over and over amidst the darkness of his strange situation, he began to wonder whether his whole experience with the crystal cube — indeed, its very existence — were not a nightmare brought on by some freakish subconscious memory of this old bit of extravagant, charlatanic reading. If so, though, the nightmare must still be in force; since his present apparently bodiless state had nothing of normality in it.

Of the time consumed by this puzzled memory and reflection, Campbell could form no estimate. Everything about his state was so unreal that ordinary dimensions and measurements became meaningless. It seemed an eternity, but perhaps it was not really long before the sudden interruption came. What happened was as strange and inexplicable as the blackness it succeeded. There was a sensation - of the mind rather than of the body — and all at once Campbell felt his thoughts swept or sucked beyond his control in tumultuous and chaotic fashion.

Memories arose irresponsibly and irrelevantly. All that he knew — all his personal background, traditions, experiences, scholarship, dreams, ideas, and inspirations-

welled up abruptly and simultaneously, with a dizzying speed and abundance which soon made him unable to keep track of any separate concept. The parade of all his mental contents became an avalanche, a cascade, a vortex. It was as horrible and vertiginous as his hypnotic flight through space when the crystal cube pulled him. Finally it sapped his consciousness and brought on fresh oblivion.

Another measureless blank—and then a slow trickle of sensation. This time it was physical, not mental. Sapphire light, and a low rumble of distant sound. There were tactile impressions—he could realise that he was lying at full length on something, though there was a baffling strangeness about the feel of his posture. He could not reconcile the pressure of the supporting surface with his own outlines—or with the outlines of the human form at all. He tried to move his arms, but found no definite response to the attempt. Instead, there were little, ineffectual nervous twitches all over the area which seemed to mark his body.

He tried to open his eyes more widely, but found himself unable to control their mechanism. The sapphire light came in a diffused, nebulous manner, and could nowhere be voluntarily focussed Into definiteness. Gradually, though, visual images began to trickle in curiously and indecisively. The limits and qualities of vision were not those which he was used to, but he could roughly correlate the sensation with what he had known as sight. As this sensation gained some degree of stability, Campbell realised that he must still be in the throes of nightmare.

He seemed to be in a room of considerable extent—of medium height, but with a large proportionate area. On every side—and he could apparently see all four sides at once—were high, narrowish slits which seemed to serve as combined doors and windows. There were singular low tables or pedestals, but no furniture of normal nature and proportions. Through the slits streamed floods of sapphire light, and beyond them could be mistily seen the sides and roofs of fantastic buildings like clustered cubes. On the walls - in the vertical panels between the slits - were strange markings of an oddly disquieting character. It was some time before Campbell understood why they disturbed him so—then he saw that they were, in repeated instances, precisely like some of the hieroglyphs on the crystal cube's disc.

The actual nightmare element, though, was something more than this. It began with the living thing which presently entered through one of the slits, advancing deliberately toward him and bearing a metal box of bizarre proportions and glassy, mirror-like surfaces. For this thing was nothing human—nothing of earth—nothing even of man's myths and dreams. It was a gigantic, pale-grey worm or centipede, as large around as a man and twice as long, with a disc-like, apparently eyeless, cilia-fringed head bearing a purple central orifice. It glided on its rear pairs of legs, with its fore part raised vertically— the legs, or at least two pairs of them, serving as arms. Along its spinal ridge was a curious purple comb, and a fan-shaped tail of some grey membrane ended its grotesque bulk. There was a ring of flexible red spikes around its neck, and from the twistings of these came clicking, twanging sounds in measured, deliberate rhythms.

Here, indeed, was outré nightmare at its height—capricious fantasy at its apex. But even this vision of delirium was not what caused George Campbell to lapse a third time into unconsciousness. It took one more thing—one final, unbearable touch—to do that. As the nameless worm advanced with its glistening box, the reclining man caught in the mirror-like surface a glimpse of what should have been his own body. Yet—horribly verifying his disordered and unfamiliar sensations—it was not his own body at all that he saw reflected in the burnished metal. It was, instead, the loathsome, pale-grey bulk of one of the great centipedes.

[Robert E. Howard]

FROM THAT FINAL LAP OF SENSELESSNESS, he emerged with a full understanding of his situation. His mind was Imprisoned in the body of a frightful native of an alien planet, while, somewhere on the other side of the universe, his own body was housing the monster's personality.

He fought down an unreasoning horror. Judged from a cosmic standpoint, why should his metamorphosis horrify him? Life and consciousness were the only realities in the universe. Form was unimportant. His present body was hideous only according to terrestrial standards. Fear and revulsion were drowned in the excitement of titanic adventure.

What was his former body but a cloak, eventually to be cast off at death anyway? He had no sentimental illusions about the life from which he had been exiled. What had it ever given him save toil, poverty, continual frustration and repression? If this life before him offered no more, at least it offered no less. Intuition told him it offered more — much more.

With the honesty possible only when life is stripped to its naked fundamentals, he realized that he remembered with pleasure only the physical delights of his former life. But he had long ago exhausted all the physical possibilities contained in that earthly body. Earth held no new thrills. But in the possession of this new, alien body he felt promises of strange, exotic joys.

A lawless exultation rose in him. He was a man without a world, tree of all conventions or inhibitions of Earth, or of this strange planet, free of every artificial restraint in the universe. He was a god! With grim amusement he thought of his body moving in earth's business and society, with all the while an alien monster staring out of the windows that were George Campbell's eyes on people who would flee !f they knew.

Let him walk the earth slaying and destroying as he would. Earth and its races no longer had any meaning to George Campbell. There he had been one of a billion nonentities, fixed in place by a mountainous accumulation of conventions, laws and manners, doomed to live and die in his sordid niche. But in one blind bound he had soared above the commonplace. This was not death, but re-birth — the birth of a full-grown mentality, with a new-found freedom that made little of physical captivity on Yekub.

He started. Yekub! It was the name of this planet, but how had he known? Then he knew, as he knew the name of him whose body he occupied- Tothe. Memory, deep grooved in Tothe's brain, was stirring in him - shadows of the knowledge Tothe had. Carved deep in the physical tissues of the brain, they spoke dimly as implanted instincts to George Campbell; and his human consciousness seized them and translated them to show him the way not only to safety and freedom, but to the power his soul, stripped to its primitive impulses, craved. Not as a slave would he dwell on Yekub, but as a king! Just as of old barbarians had sat on the throne of lordly empires.

For the first time he turned his attention to his surroundings. He still lay on the couch-like thing in the midst of that fantastic room, and the centipede man stood before him, holding the polished metal object, and clashing its neck-spikes. Thus it spoke to him, Campbell knew, and what it said he dimly understood, through the implanted thought processes of Tothe, just as he knew the creature was Yukth, supreme lord of science.

But Campbell gave no heed, for he had made his desperate plan, a plan so alien to the ways of Yekub that !t was beyond Yukth's comprehension and caught him wholly unprepared. Yukth, like Campbell, saw the sharp-pointed metal shard on a nearby table, but to Yukth it was only a scientific implement. He did not even know it could be used as a weapon. Campbell's earthly mind supplied the knowledge and the action that followed, driving Tothe's body into movements no man of Yekub had ever made before.

Campbell snatched the pointed shard and struck, ripping savagely upward. Yukth reared and toppled, his entrails spilling on the floor. In an instant Campbell was streaking for a door. His speed was amazing, exhilarating, first fulfilment of the promise of novel physical sensations.

As he ran, guided wholly by the Instinctive knowledge implanted in Tothe's physical reflexes, it was as If he were borne by a separate consciousness in his legs. Tothe's body was bearing him along a route it had traversed ten thousand times when animated by Tothe's mind.

Down a winding corridor he raced, up a twisted stair, through a carved door, and the same instincts that had brought him there told him he had found what he sought. He was in a circular room with a domed roof from which shone a livid blue light. A strange structure rose In the middle of the rainbow-hued floor, tier on tier, each of a separate, vivid color. The ultimate tier was a purple cone, from the apex of which a blue smoky mist drifted upward to a sphere that poised in mid-air—a sphere that shone like translucent ivory.

This, the deep-grooved memories of Tothe told Campbell, was the god of Yekub, though why the people of Yekub feared and worshipped it had been forgotten a million years. A worm-priest stood between him and the altar which no hand of flesh had ever touched. That it could be touched was a blasphemy that had never occurred to a man of Yekub. The worm-priest stood in frozen horror until Campbell's shard ripped the life out of him.

On his centipede-legs Campbell clambered the tiered altar, heedless of its sudden quiverings, heedless of the change that was taking place in the floating sphere, heedless of the smoke that now billowed out In blue clouds. He was drunk with the feel of power. He feared the superstitions of Yekub no more than he feared those of earth. With that globe in his hands he would be king of Yekub. The worm men would dare deny him nothing, when he held their god as hostage. He reached a hand for the ball—no longer ivory-hued, but red as blood...

[Frank Belknap Long]

OUT OF THE TENT INTO THE PALE AUGUST NIGHT walked the body of George Campbell. It moved with a slow, wavering gait between the bodies of enormous trees, over a forest path strewed with sweet scented pine needles. The air was crisp and cold. The sky was an inverted bowl of frosted silver flecked with stardust, and far to the north the Aurora Borealis splashed streamers of fire.

The head of the walking man lolled hideously from side to side. From the corners of his lax mouth drooled thick threads of amber froth, which fluttered in the night breeze. He walked upright at first, as a man would walk, but gradually as the tent receded, his posture altered. His torso began almost imperceptibly to slant, and his limbs to shorten.

In a far-off world of outer space the centipede creature that was George Campbell clasped to Its bosom a god whose lineaments were red as blood, and ran with insect-like quiverings across a rainbow-hued hall and out through massive portals into the bright glow of alien suns.

Weaving between the trees of earth in an attitude that suggested the awkward loping of a werebeast, the body of George Campbell was fulfilling a mindless destiny. Long, claw-tipped fingers dragged leaves from a carpet of odorous pine needles as it moved toward a wide expanse of gleaming water.

In the far-off, extra-galactic world of the worm people, George Campbell moved between cyclopean blocks of black masonry down long, fern-planted avenues holding aloft the round red god.

There was a harsh animal cry in the underbrush near the gleaming lake on earth where the mind of a worm creature dwelt in a body swayed by instinct. Human teeth sank into soft animal fur, tore at black animal flesh. A little silver fox sank its fangs in frantic retaliation into a furry human wrist, and thrashed about in terror as its blood spurted. Slowly the body of George Campbell arose, its mouth splashed with fresh blood. With upper limbs swaying oddly it moved towards the waters of the lake.

As the variform creature that was George Campbell crawled between the black blocks of stone thousands of worm-shapes prostrated themselves in the scintillating dust before it. A godlike power seemed to emanate from its weaving body as it moved with a slow, undulant motion toward a throne of spiritual empire transcending all the sovereignties of earth.

A trapper stumbling wearily through the dense woods of earth near the tent where the worm-creature dwelt in the body of George Campbell came to the gleaming waters of the lake and discerned something dark floating there. He had been lost in the woods all night, and weariness enveloped him like a leaden cloak in the pale morning light.

But the shape was a challenge that he could not ignore. Moving to the edge of the water he knelt in the soft mud and reached out toward the floating bulk. Slowly he pulled it to the shore.

Far off in outer space the worm-creature holding the glowing red god ascended a throne that gleamed like the constellation Cassiopeia under an alien vault of hyper-suns. The great deity that he held aloft energized his worm tenement, burning away in the white fire of a supermundane spirituality all animal dross.

On earth the trapper gazed with unutterable horror into the blackened and hairy face of the drowned man. It was a bestial face, repulsively anthropoid in contour, and from its twisted, distorted mouth black ichor poured.

"He who sought your body in the abysses of Time will occupy an unresponsive tenement," said the red god. "No spawn of Yekub can control the body of a human.

177

"On all earth, living creatures rend one another, and feast with unutterable cruelty on their kith and kin. No worm-mind can control a bestial man-body when it yearns to raven. Only man-minds Instinctively conditioned through the course of ten thousand generations can keep the human instincts in thrall. Your body will destroy Itself on earth, seeking the blood of its animal kin, seeking the cool water where it can wallow at Its ease. Seeking eventually destruction, for the death-instinct is more powerful in it than the instincts of life and it will destroy itself in seeking to return to the slime from which it sprang."

Thus spoke the round red god of Yekub in a far-off segment of the space-time continuum to George Campbell as the latter, with all human desire purged away, sat on a throne and ruled an empire of worms more wisely kindly, and benevolently than any man of earth had ever ruled an empire of men.

THE WHITE ROAD[1]

CHAPTER I. GATE OF THE WHITE ROAD

DAVID CORFAX LAID DOWN the last torn sheet of the stained old parchment with a wonder that had grown steadily while he read. What he had read was incredible, but the true incredibility lay in that it had been written. Therein was the. heart of his wonder and the indefinable terror of it. For what the writing dealt with was—the White Road!

All his life he had known the White Road. You saw it first as a slit, a hair-line of white light, just the width of your eyes and somewhere, it seemed behind them— somewhere between your brain and your eyes, in your own head. In childhood, it had been after you had gone to bed; sometimes as soon as your lids closed, sometimes when you were dropping off to sleep. Later it might come in broad daylight, while you sat thinking or reading. But at those times you never got far on the White Road.

The laws of this world not those of yours.

---

[1] *EDITOR'S NOTE: These last 2 items are fragments that Merritt left unfinished at his death.*

All his life he had known the White Road; in all his life he had spoken of it only to three persons. Two of these were dead; the third had been a child whom he had not seen for years and who should long ago have forgotten. Yet it had been she who had sent him the parchment. And out of it had come a voice silent four hundred years, and speaking of the White Road as one who had been a pilgrim upon it.

How young he had been when first he saw the White Road, David Corfax could not tell. But it was as real to him as was this old house in which he sat, the sun of a September afternoon streaming through the window upon this yellowed manuscript which told him that the White Road was no dream — or if a dream then not his alone.

And there had been that enigmatic postscript of Deborah's: "I too have seen the White Road!"

Was it real after all? Whether real or not, it had its mechanics, unchanging, unchangeable. First there was the humming, not heard but felt, a vibration along every nerve, in every cell. Then the slit, the hair-line of white light.

Then the slit would open — half an inch, an inch. And then the White Road would begin to unroll. You could see straight ahead of you, but that was all. It was as though you stood a little distance back of the slit.

In a sort of black box that moved smoothly along the road. And yet you seemed to be out on the road, too. Sometimes the sides would sweep past swiftly, as though you were galloping on some effortlessly moving horse; sometimes slowly as though you were walking. But once the road began to unroll you never stopped. And you never looked back, that is until you learned that looking back meant journey's end. When you stopped, the slit went out—like a light and you were back in your room. You looked back into your room. When you turned, the road was gone.

Nor could you control the motion with which you went, nor could you, try as you would, by any effort of will cause the window that opened on the road to appear. It was there, without warning—or it was not. Nor could he ever remember clearly what he had seen when on the White Road. The road itself was always plain—wide and smoothly paved, sometimes straight sometimes curving, going on and on and on. There were people, but of what kind he never remembered. There were forests, colorful and flowered...a towering range of mountains, strangely serrated, toothed, pinnacled...enormously high, purple and amethyst and looking as though they had been cut from cardboard...no distance to them and with garlands of little suns circling their peaks...there was a city of domes and minarets...beside a purple sea. And there were things that terrified...that had been in childhood when he had learned to look back to escape them. Later, he faced them...but could not remember, waking, what he had faced. Memory of music...like Sibelius.

The road appeared without warning? No, there was always the humming that preceded it. It was a strange sound, not heard but felt. It seemed to vibrate through him, and as it did so his body became weightless. He could not feel the bed he lay in if he clenched his hands he could not feel the fingers…the humming seemed to deaden all nerves of touch. It grew louder, swifter rather rising in vibrancy rather than in pitch as the slit widened. He remembered, ah, there was one thing he remembered clearly enough. One night the humming had quickened and the slit had opened wider than ever before—or since. And over it, like a climber, a woman's hand, long-fingered, yellow as old ivory had clawed with talons like a condor had crept. And two unwinking, amber eyes had glared into his. He remembered how he had screamed, and his mother had come to him, and he could see today the fright, the numb horror, that had appeared upon her face when he had wept and sobbed about the White Road…he had been no more than six then. He remembered.

When you looked back, and the road came again, you had to begin at the beginning. But if you could hold your nerve, and not look back, after a while you went to sleep. Then, if the dream came again the next night, as sometimes it did, you would go on from where you had stopped the night before. That was how he had gotten as far as sight of the strange city beside the purple sea. Three nights he had been on the road. Yes, there was some system, some law governing it.

There was a dark: road too. That was an evil road. Even in childhood he knew that it came close to the White Road and was to be avoided. But later, he felt a pull as he put it, to this road. And often yielded. He could see nothing on this, could only hear voices. And he must go so gently, so quietly. There was a hill, and behind it the murmur of voices, the creaking of stays, the sounds of a port. He knew it was a hill, because it loomed blackly against a faintly red sky, as though there were fires burning. He knew that he must never look over that hill, never go over it or he would be utterly lost. Could never return.

Then his mother had died. He had gone through boarding school, through college, become a wanderer. Two years on the desert.

When Old Gods Wake

Chapter I. Altar of Kukulkan

THE SILENCE SEEMED TO BE FOCUSED within the temple; to have its heart there; a heart that did not need to beat, since all the silence was alive. Outside the heat of the Yucatan midday held the ruins in breathless grip. Barry Manson, crouching at the base of the ancient altar, thought: the silence…marched…marched into the temple. The shrieks of the parrots were cut off first…then the little blue and yellow birds stopped quarreling in the crimson fruited tree at the base of the shattered stairway…and then the silence marched up the stairway and into this chamber and crowded against the seaward side…and that shut out the swish of the waves.

He looked at Joan. She sat a few paces away, her back against the massive pedestal of a broken pillar. Her hands were clasped around her knees. Her eyes were intent upon the wall behind the altar. A painting once had covered that wall. The fingers of time, working patiently through the centuries, had plucked away most of the stucco that had carried it. But above the altar, as though protected by its shadow, a large and irregular fragment remained. Upon it, colors still vivid, Were the head and shoulders of

Kukulkan, God of the Air of the ancient Mayans—and much more than that.

The Feathered Serpent, his symbol and his avatar, floated over him, fanged jaws agape, plumed wings spread wide. The face of Kukulkan was the conventionalized one of the New Empire; the nose grotesquely lengthened like that of a tapir, lips thick and protruding, prognathous-jawed, bat-eared; the ears ringed and the labret through the nostrils; head plumed with the sacred panacho.

The painted gaze of the god seemed fixed as intently upon the girl as hers upon him.

The pedestal against which Joan leaned was covered with carved figures of priests of Kukulkan who had served him when ruined Tuloom had been one of the great cities of the Mayans, and this its holiest temple. On these figures the colors were also bright. Into them Joan's copper hair melted, merged with their reds and ochres so that for an instant Barry had the illusion that her face was all of her.

A disembodied face peering out of the stone and holding communion with the god like a summoned priestess.

Impatiently Barry arose and walked over to her. She did not look up. She whispered, eyes still absorbed by the painted god:

"Don't break the silence, Barry! It's like the silence that wraps the city of Jade...where the thousand sages of T'zan T'zao sit holding fast to the thought that created the world…and that the ghost of a ghost of a sound would destroy…and with it the world…"

He felt increase of revolt against the fantasies gathering about him. He shook his shoulders and laughed. He said, loudly:

"The silence is broken, Joan—and the world still spins."

It was true. The silence was broken. It was retreating from the chamber, slowly…marching away as it had marched in. Faintly came the swish of the waves, growing ever stronger. The silence was marching out of the chamber toward the shattered stairway up which it had come. Joan arose, slowly…it was odd, Barry thought, how every movement of hers in rising kept to the rhythm, kept to the beat, of the unseen and unheard feet of the retreating silence.

The silence marched down the stairway. He heard again the quarreling of the little blue and yellow birds…then the shrieks of the parrots…

Joan said, unsteadily: "It was time you did that, Barry. It was…doing things to me. Look, Barry—look……!"

He followed her finger, pointing to the painted face of Kukulkan. For a breath he saw it…another face looking out from the wall.

An ageless face…the nose long and curved and delicate. The lips full but sharply cut, archaically sensuous…hair as red as his own and eyes as blue as. Joan's. A face as devoid of human equivalence as it was timeless…yet human…as though the seed from which it had sprung into godhood had been human. Incalculable, unreadable…but still within it something that could be read up to that point where the humanness of it merged into the god…might be read more plainly if the god would within it merge more fully into the humanness. Nothing of benevolence in it…but neither was there shade of malevolence, cruelty…humanless, in human mask.

Barry thought: it is like that mountain peak in the City of Jade of which Joan spoke…the peak shaped like the head of a man and all of clearest crystal to which the thoughts of men are drawn…all their thoughts…and pass from its eyes and mouth cleansed of falsehood and of error, prejudice and hatred and love…standing naked and stark before T'zan T'zao to be judged…

Power was in the face, immense power…and something of wildness, of freedom…the freedom of primæval things…like the wind, the waves, the sun…

And then the face was gone. Upon the wall was the tapir snout of Kukulkan, the protruding lips, the fanged and feathered serpent.

His hand was clenching Joan's wrist. She whispered:

"You saw it! You're hurting me!"

He dropped her wrist. He said: "It is another painting beneath this one. An older painting. Some trick of the light brought it out."

She said, doubtful: "Maybe. But I think it was Kukulkan as the first Mayans knew him. Kukulkan who came to them from still an older race. Kukulkan when he was worshipped with flowers and fruits and incense and prayer. Before his worship was debased and the cruel human sacrifices began. That was when and why he turned from the Mayans. And so their doom came swiftly upon them. For it was never he who came to them thereafter, Barry. It was an evil god hiding behind his mask and name—"

She hesitated, seemed listening: "But yes—he did come. Came even to the Aztecs, who steeped his rites in even greater cruelties and renamed him Quetzalcoatl...came again and again to thwart that other god when his evil grew too strong...the Lord of Darkness, the Lord of the Dead... "

Her voice died; she stood with eyes rapt, face colorless, bent as though listening. He took her by the shoulders, shook her:

"Snap out of it, Joan. What's the matter with you? You're talking nonsense."

"Am I, Barry? It was what Kukulkan was telling me."

She dropped her head on his shoulder; clung to him, trembling. His hands slipped from her shoulders, drew her to him. He said huskily:

"Coming any closer to loving me, Joan?"

She raised her eyes to his frankly, yet with something of regret lurking in them.

"Sorry, Barry dear. But it's still the same. I— "

He interrupted her, speaking monotonously: "Like you better than any other man I know, except Bill, of course, and I wish I could love you the way you want, but—yes, Joan, I know all that by heart now."

She flushed and said: "That's not fair. After all, Bill's my brother and why shouldn't I love him? And I do like you better than anyone else. So much so that at times—" she stopped; he repeated eagerly:

"That at times?"

"Never mind. Barry, why do you want me? There are plenty of nice girls who like just the things you do. I know a dozen who would love you—and any one of them would make you a perfect wife. I don't like the 'things you do. Or if I do, to me they're only brief amusements. Why, I'd rather help Bill dig up a cup from some ruin that spans the gap of knowledge between its maker and us than win a thousand sporting trophies."

He said: "If you loved me that wouldn't make any difference."

She shook her head: "We've been brought up differently, Barry—and we're both too set in our ways to change. I am anyway..." Suddenly she laughed:

"And you haven't fooled me by this trip, Barry Manson. I know damned well that it wasn't any abrupt interest in the Mayans that prompted it. I'm mighty grateful to you for giving Bill the chance he's always wanted. But I wouldn't marry you out of gratitude, and I don't think you'd want me to — would you, Barry?"

His gray eyes narrowed: he said, brutally: "Listen, redhead. You don't fool me any either. It's damned little of highbrow or blue-stocking you'd be if you fell in love with a man. Nature didn't build you that way. And it would be damned little you'd be thinking of fossils if that happened. You'd be too busy having babies."

She said, coldly: "I think that's rather — beastly!" He said, hotly: "Is that so? What's beastly about babies? You'd be getting a slant on the present day with some outlook on the future — instead of burying your red head in the past. What I'm afraid of is that you'll marry some dusty-dry, mummy-minded, scientific grave robber and spend the rest of your life nursing fossils instead of what you are obviously designed for — "

She interrupted, furiously, eyes snapping blue sparks:

"I'll let nobody pick my husband! Least of all — you!"

"Won't you!" Barry's too-quick anger flared. "It seems to me you were ready enough to pick wives for me just now. Not one but a dozen — " He gripped her arms and swung her to him. "You — the highbrow scientist? Like hell you are! Look at that mop of red hair. Those eyes of yours with the devil's twist to the ends of them, that mouth of yours—and I've seen you in your rag of a bathing suit! I tell you again, by God, that once you're awake it's not fossils you'll be thinking of! And maybe this will help wake you—"

He held her close, kissed eyes and throat, pressed his lips to hers. She lay in his arms, passive, unresisting. She said at last, indifferently:

"Cave-man stuff, Barry. Too crude. It doesn't interest me at all."

He released her, stepping back as though out of a dash of cold water. She raised her arms and began to coil her disordered hair. She laughed at him, a little too sweetly— though he did not know it.

"You see, Barry dear, we're as far apart as the poles. You make love to me by enumerating my—ah, charms, is the cliché for it, I think. You are an—ah, anatomical lover. It is a viewpoint, certainly. A Sultan's viewpoint, but I do not care for Sultans. Nor," went on Joan, still far too sweetly and reasonably, "do I think that my worthinesses are wholly anatomical. But then—you've always been rich—"

~ **THE END** ~

More stories from Abraham Merritt...

Through the Dragon Glass, 2011, ISBN: 9781849023191

Includes the short stories Through the Dragon Class, The People of the Pit and Three lines of Old French.

The Ship of Ishtar, 2011, ISBN: 9781849025300

A fantasy tale of adventure.

Burn Witch Burn!, 2011,
ISBN: 9781849025478

A classic with elements of
fantasy and mystery. This
novel inspired the movie
"Devil Doll".

Dwellers in the Mirage,
2011, ISBN: 9781849025348

A science fantasy novel in
which a war between two
races is begun by an evil
spirit.

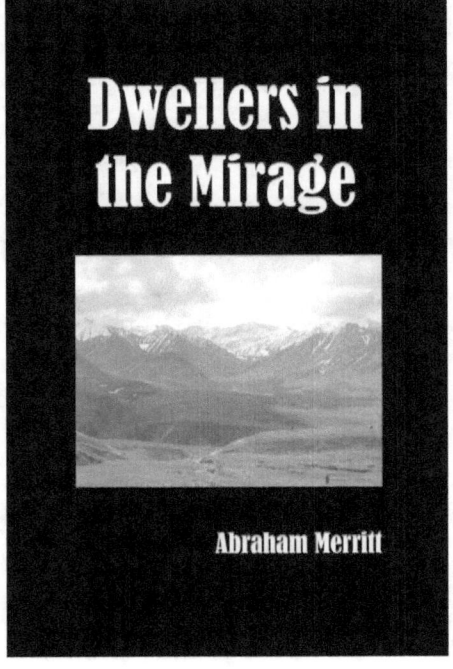